ALWAYS A GENTLEMAN, NEVER A DUKE

JESSIE CLEVER

SOMEDAY LADY
PUBLISHING, LLC.

ALWAYS A GENTLEMAN, NEVER A DUKE

Published by Someday Lady Publishing, LLC

Copyright © 2024 by Jessica McQuaid

All rights reserved.

No part of this book may be reproduced in any form or by any electronic or mechanical means, including information storage and retrieval systems, without written permission from the author, except for the use of brief quotations in a book review.

This book is a work of fiction. Any references to historical events, real people, or real places are used fictitiously. Other names, characters, places and events are products of the author's imagination, and any resemblances to actual events or places or persons, living or dead, is entirely coincidental.

NO AI TRAINING: Without in any way limiting the author's [and publisher's] exclusive rights under copyright, any use of this publication to "train" generative artificial intelligence (AI) technologies to generate text is expressly prohibited.

ISBN-13: 979-8-9881916-7-4

For Judy.
I still don't know the difference between further and farther, but I do know you've always got my back. Thank you. For everything.

CHAPTER 1

*L*ady Eloise Bounds wanted to say something achingly romantic about the night they first met, something about how they were drawn together by moonlight. And while they did, in fact, meet under the moon, she was fairly certain at the time he was a ghoul come to steal her soul, and there was nothing at all romantic about that.

She grabbed a branch of the nearest bush, as if its beleaguered limbs held impenctrable power, and pulled it in front of her to shield her body.

"Stop!" Her voice was loud in the quiet of the night, and she cringed, her eyes going up to the empty and dark windows that surrounded the Mayfair courtyard into which she had slipped only minutes before, certain at any moment that light would appear in one of them and she would be caught. She had gone to so much trouble to escape the house without raising alarm, and now she had nearly given herself away with a cry of fright. For she was frightened.

The creature that stood in front of her appeared to have the qualities of a man, but his eyes glowed red like a demon. She was not of the spiritual sort and hardly of the religious sort, so for her mind to instantly assume the creature in front of her to be of demonic origin spoke to just how ghoulish he appeared.

He held up his hands then, hands that looked perfectly human. She could tell because he wasn't wearing gloves, and the moonlight traced each curve of finger as an artist might use a brush against the canvas, highlighting just the right bits for maximum effect. Her heart thundered in her chest, and her arms shook so that the leaves of the limb she still held clenched in her hands rustled, and yet she felt the odd romantic stirring at the sight of his long fingers.

"I won't hurt you." His voice was soft, much calmer than hers had been, and he kept his hands pushed out in front of him as though to reassure her.

"That's precisely what someone with nefarious intent would say."

His hands faltered, and there was the suggestion of a smile in his voice, but the shadows around him were too thick for her to be certain if he did indeed smile. "Do you often encounter gentlemen with nefarious intent at midnight in a Mayfair courtyard?"

"I don't know that you're a gentleman." She pulled the limb closer to her chest, bracing it just beneath her chin.

His head tilted ever so much before he began to lower his hands. "If I may," he said, but his hands kept moving before she gave permission, and she watched him carefully.

He took a step toward her, and she pushed the limb away from her like a sword. He stopped immediately, hands once more in the air, and silence vibrated between them. He didn't advance though, and after a moment, his hands started to lower again.

Her heart pounded, but the limb had stopped shaking, and she wondered why. Why did this stranger with demon eyes cause such calm to wash over her?

She realized then that he wasn't coming at her, but rather shifting so he was in moonlight instead of shadow, and finally she saw the truth of it.

"Oh." The word was sad and hollow, and she felt just a little repulsed at her disappointment. Had she been *hoping* the man was a ghoul?

Instead he was incredibly ordinary, and the demon eyes were merely a pair of railway spectacles in which the lenses had been swapped for what appeared to be red glass.

She could see his smile now, and she found it to be absurdly boyish. Something hiccupped inside of her, and she pressed a hand to her stomach in surprise.

No. No, it couldn't be happening. Not like this. The thing for which she had endured two painfully boring seasons couldn't come now. Not when she had resigned herself to her fate.

"I feel as though I've disappointed you somehow." His voice was boyish to match his smile, and she wished she could see his face more clearly, but the spectacles obstructed her view. "I'm usually in a person's presence for quite a great deal longer before I do that."

She tried to stop her own smile, suddenly worried she would give too much of herself away, but she didn't know why she would think that. This man was a perfect stranger.

She pointed to the railway spectacles. "May I ask what those are for? You're not precisely on a train at the moment."

He made a self-deprecating noise then and pulled the spectacles from his face.

Oh lud. His face was boyish too.

His features were clear in the moonlight, but somehow she knew her heart would recognize him even if her eyes could not. He had light brown hair that stuck up haphazardly around the crown of his head as though he had spent a great deal of time adjusting the spectacles, and he hadn't bothered to fix the damage they'd done to his hair. His forehead was high, his eyes twinkling with mirth much as his boyish smile suggested a private joke, and his jaw was surprisingly firm, almost chiseled. While the man oozed the suggestion of fun, she sensed something strong beneath the surface, and it called to her.

She heard a strange rustling noise in her ears and realized her hand had started to shake once more, and as she still held the limb, it gave her away. She noticed his eyes fall to the limb the moment hers did, and she snatched her hand back, putting it behind her as if to hide it.

He held up the spectacles and thankfully answered her question without mention of the shaking limb. "It's a new design I had hoped to test tonight, but the clouds keep getting in my way." He held the spectacles across one open palm as he pointed to the sides of the lens where normally there would have been mesh to protect the wearer's eyes from flying hot coals and found the mesh had been replaced by cut tin. "I've modified the typical railway spectacle to better shelter the eye from outside light and focus the eye's attention on what's in front of the viewer." Now he pointed to the red lenses. "The red is a theory of mine. I propose red light helps sustain a person's night vision, allowing them to take in the night sky."

Her eyes flew to his face. "You're stargazing."

It wasn't a question, and she wondered why her voice sounded so breathless.

He blinked, his lips moving without sound for a moment. "I suppose I am. Although rather inadvertently. The main purpose of my excursion tonight is to test the red glass." He held the spectacles aloft. "Should you like to try them? I would value your input."

She was momentarily startled by the forward gesture, but if she'd had presence of mind, she'd realize everything about their encounter was forward. Her hand was already reaching for the spectacles when she snatched it back.

"I don't even know your name." The words left her lips in a kind of shocked whisper as she momentarily realized what was happening.

She was alone with a gentleman in the dark of a midnight courtyard. It was utterly scandalous, and should they be caught, everything would be ruined. Her mother—Oh God, Eloise's mother would be lost to hysterics. So much planning had gone into this season, and they'd even managed to arrive in town early, and here Eloise was, cavorting with a stranger in the dark.

"It's Tuck." He said it so casually she almost missed it.

"I'm sorry?"

"Tuck," he repeated and then smiled sheepishly. "Short for Tucker."

It wasn't proper. The way he said his name and the introduction. The whole thing should have been conducted by a mutual acquaintance in public with lots of prying eyes that would keep everything in check.

But then she found herself saying, "Eloise."

Tuck smiled that heart-tugging smile and said, "Eloise. It's a pleasure to meet you. I hope you won't mind very much playing the part of my research assistant."

She snatched up the spectacles before she could think about the way her stomach fluttered when he looked at her like that. She pushed the spectacles onto her nose, hooking the bent arms around her ears, and peered skyward.

"I can't see anything." It was true. The light of the gas lamp above the door she had slipped out of not minutes before obstructed the view of the night sky.

"Allow me."

He touched her before she knew what he was about. He gripped her elbows through the heavy weight of her cloak and drew her back into the darkness along the path where she had first discovered him lingering. The heat that seared through so many layers was startling, but it hardly compared to the heat that coursed through her body when her back met his chest as he stopped abruptly.

He was much taller than she had first thought, and she found herself tucked neatly against him. Her eyes widened behind the glass lenses, but she saw nothing, her mind too clouded with the sudden realization of her dangerous position. Oh God, it felt incredible. The whole length of his body was pressed against hers, and suddenly her heart thudded with something too perilous to name.

This.

This was why she hadn't accepted a single proposal in her two seasons. This was why she had held out. This was why her mother was so horribly frustrated with her. Tears sprang to her eyes at the terribleness of it, and she was glad for the spectacles. Tears because it was too late. She had already resigned herself to what lay ahead of her, finally abandoning her notion that her marriage might be different. That she might obtain the rarest of things among society.

A love match.

Two seasons were two seasons too many, and now there were two dukes on the marriage mart. Two dukes seeking wives, and three Bounds daughters against all the other debutantes society had to offer.

She closed her eyes, willing the tears to abate. It hadn't mattered in the last two seasons. Eloise's older sister, Gwendolyn, was firmly and seemingly happily on the shelf while her next oldest sister, Annie, had found love only to have it snatched away again, donning a widow's weeds and finding solace in her grief. But now, none of the Bounds sisters were safe, and Eloise had given up her fanciful notion of love.

But that was all before she'd stumbled upon a man with red eyes in the middle of a dark courtyard.

"Is that better?"

His warm breath skated across her ear, and it was all she could do not to sigh with pleasure. But it brought her back to the present, and she opened her eyes, sucking in a breath now.

"Oh." It was all she could say. The stars were tiny pinpricks of light against the inky black, so much more defined than with the naked eye. "Oh, I think you might be right."

His laugh was soft against her ear. "You sound surprised."

She spun about, suddenly wishing to reassure him that she wasn't doubting his intelligence, but she found him smiling, and she felt rather foolish standing there in the red spectacles. Carefully she slipped them from her face and handed them to him.

"I *was* surprised actually," she said. "It's not often we debutantes have a chance to stargaze. It's mostly needlepoint and watercolors."

For the first time since she had encountered him, the smile slipped from his lips. "Eloise." He spoke her name carefully, and the heady warmth she had felt standing in his arms began to fade. "I know why it is I'm standing out here on a cold, dark night, but I failed to ask you why you're here."

Her lips parted, the need to tell him everything raw and inexplicable in her chest. But how could she tell him? How could she tell this stranger that she had waited two seasons to feel anything for a man, and now she felt entirely too much when it was too late?

She couldn't. So instead she said, "I suppose I was looking for a moment of respite before I begin the season tomorrow." She fingered the velvet of her cloak, distracting herself from her beating heart with the softness of the fabric. When she looked up again, she found a hint of sadness in his puzzled expression that had her wondering.

He nodded. "I can understand that all too well. I think tomorrow is the start of something for many people in London. Even if we're not all searching for the same thing."

It was such a cryptic statement her mind couldn't form a proper response before he was already bidding her good night.

He gave a formal bow that was rather funny in the circumstances, and she forgot the sadness she had seen in his face only seconds before.

"Good night, Eloise," he said. His smile returned to his face, and she wondered when it had become familiar to her, a thought that only gave her more pain.

"Good night, Tuck," she said.

It wasn't until later when she was lying sleepless in bed that she wondered just what a man like Tuck could be searching for.

* * *

"Do you know I don't think I've ever been to a ball?" The Honorable Mr. Tucker Ryan stood next to his cousin, Liam Capshaw, the Duke of Ardley, the following night, trying not to think about how much more enjoyable his adventures of the previous night had been. "Assemblies, yes, of course. Plenty of those in Derbyshire. But no balls."

Liam's gaze remained riveted to the other side of the room even as he said, "I promise this is where you want to be tonight, cousin. Despite the crush that it is." He finally pulled his gaze away. "You must remind me though to introduce you to the gentlemen in the cards room. That is where you'll find your most lucrative prospects."

Tuck watched as his cousin's eyes dimmed slightly, and he headed off what he knew would be the same plea his cousin had given him for the past four days since Tuck had arrived in town.

"You know I will not allow it. We've been over this. While the coffers of the Ardley title are deep, they are not enough to fund the expedition I have in mind." He gestured to the room around them. "That is why a pool of investors is necessary."

Liam's expression turned dismal. "You know I would give you the funds without question."

"And bankrupt the title?"

A line appeared between Liam's brows. "You think so little of the Ardley title?"

Tuck laughed at Liam's pontificating tone. Tuck's and Liam's mothers were sisters, and Tuck had missed the weighty title of a dukedom by just that much. So it was that Tuck was a mere mister—practically poor with a pitiful allowance granted him by his father—to his cousin's much loftier position.

Although it was impossible to tell there was any difference in rank between them. Tuck and Liam had been like brothers since childhood, and nothing had really changed when Liam assumed the title upon his father's death, and it remained a relationship Tuck treasured above all else. Even his research.

"I suppose you already have prospects for yourself in mind," Tuck said, carefully turning the subject away from himself and the daunting challenge that had brought him to London.

He had been happy in Oxford, squirreling away the days in the Bodleian, lost in pages of research so ancient and priceless he could almost imagine how gold prospectors of America's Wild West might feel. But as it often happened with book research, he had met a dead end, an obstacle only to be conquered with practical research.

Practical research meant money.

The very thing Tuck did not have.

But there were plenty of people in London who had it, and so he had come on an invitation from his cousin, and here he was.

Out of the library and into the masses in the name of money.

God, he had never felt more uncomfortable.

For a brief moment, he remembered her, the stranger he had met in the dark. Such an oddly magical interlude in what was going to be, he knew, an arduous and uncomfortable endeavor, and he took comfort in the memory of his unexpected encounter.

Would he see her again? Might there be more than a chance encounter?

He hadn't much to commend him, and the lady was likely exactly that, a lady and therefore out of his reach. He was of refined birth, and his connection to the Duke of Ardley elevated him above many, but he was still without title and possessing of only modest means. It didn't matter just then. The memory of his midnight encounter soothed him, and he found himself calming even as his challenge loomed before him.

He needed funding if he were to ever uncover the deadly secrets in the aurora borealis and why they held the power to disrupt crucial telegraph communication. He must discover their powers, or he would never find solace, not after what had happened, and more he would never be able to stop the tragedy from occurring again.

Before he could allow his thoughts to pull him deeper into darkness, he turned to Liam to find his cousin tugging his cuffs into place as though preparing for the firing squad.

"I have selected several debutantes from good families that may be suitable, yes, but I hardly see how that should curtail my usual activities," he said.

Tuck refrained from rolling his eyes. It would do no good as his cousin was the consummate flirt. Not a rogue in any way, Liam never took his dalliances with the opposite sex quite so far. It was merely that his cousin enjoyed their company, and even more, his effect on them.

Tuck almost admired him. Liam's approach to flirtation would make any man of science proud.

"And I take it you're about to introduce yourself to one such prospect?" Tuck eyed his cousin as the man fixed his hair.

"Something like that." His cousin stepped forward and jostled a short matronly woman engaged in conversation just to their left. "Birdie, dear girl, do an old chap a favor."

The woman turned owlish eyes on Liam that were piqued with irritation, but the irritation melted away when realization dawned on the woman's face. Tuck shook his head and looked away. Still, he heard the exchange quite clearly.

"Liam, darling, anything for you. You know that," cooed the woman.

Tuck could picture Liam's smile as he said, "I require an introduction. Might you be in a position to help?"

Tuck heard a shuffling, and curiosity won out. He turned to find the woman had left her huddle of matrons and stepped closer to Liam, her fan tapping the duke's arm familiarly.

"If I'm unable to offer one, I shall find someone who can. Who is it that has caught your attention?" The woman had thin lips marked by deep creases Tuck knew had come from years of making the pursed expression she did just then, her eyebrows lifting in the center, lips coming together in question as she waited for Liam's response.

"Stoke Bruerne. Have you a connection?"

The woman called Birdie twittered like one. "Oh, of course, darling. Everyone who is anyone has a connection with Nancy. That's the countess, dear. Follow me." The woman waved a gloved hand, her fingers adorned with countless jewels that jockeyed for space on her diminutive digits.

Liam turned to him with a raised eyebrow, and Tuck shrugged. He had no desire to plunge into the fray as of yet, and so he followed his cousin as he in turn followed Birdie. Although short and narrow or perhaps because of it, the woman slipped easily through the crowd, tossing an *excuse me* here and a *pardon* there. They soon emerged on the opposite side of the room where refreshment tables had been set up along the perimeter, and clusters of ladies and gentlemen hovered in the relative calm so far removed from the dance floor.

"Wait here," Birdie said with a wave of her hand as she toddled through the space to one cluster in particular to their right.

"Stoke Bruerne?" Tuck said in the interim. "I suppose the family offers a gaggle of ladies to choose from?" He infused the remark with sarcasm. There was nothing he disliked more than the way society forced ladies of a certain age to parade themselves about as if they were horseflesh before the auctioneer.

Liam nodded though as if he were in the market. Tuck supposed the man was and felt almost sorry for him.

"The youngest one," Liam said. "Ellen? Ellie? Elaine? Something like that."

Tuck held back a grimace. "You seem invested."

Liam gave a one-shouldered shrug. "As invested as I can be at this point." His eyes scanned the crowd like prey waiting for its predator to spring out of the bushes. "I have certain responsibilities to the title, and yet every marrying mama is too eager to throw her eligible daughter at my feet without considering the girl's feelings in the matter and my own responsibilities."

When worded like that, Tuck could almost feel the noose of the dukedom and was once more glad he had escaped it.

"And the youngest Stoke Bruerne daughter meets your requirements?"

Liam nodded, his gaze moving back to Birdie who was speaking animatedly to a tall woman in a dark green gown, pearls at her throat. "The eldest Stoke Bruerne daughter would have been more suitable, but her father managed to marry her off only this morning, and the second eldest is a widow." He turned to Tuck, his face grim. "I don't dally with widows. You never know when you're going to find one who actually loved her dear, departed husband, and worships the ghost of the man she has made perfect in her memory." He shook his head, his eyes traveling back to Birdie. "No, it's only the youngest one that will do."

Tuck raised both eyebrows. "Your deductions make you sound like a scientist. Careful, cousin, or I shall think you plan to tread on my accolades."

Liam turned with a wicked grin tipping up one side of his mouth. "Should you ever achieve any."

The barb was good natured, and Tuck couldn't help but smile. Tuck had missed this. Their boyhoods had allowed them to play together, grow together. Fortune had them both attending Eton, and their camaraderie continued. It was only at Oxford that their differences became apparent. Liam took a course of education that would prepare him to be a gentleman and a duke while Tuck had sought a more rigorous study that might lend him to a profession.

And answers.

He watched as Birdie gestured behind her, and Liam shifted beside him.

"Say something," he muttered.

Tuck started. "Uh, the term aurora comes from the Roman. Aurora. Goddess of the dawn. She was believed to have journeyed from the east to the west to herald the arrival of the sun. The Greek used the term Eos for the goddess, but really Eos Borealis doesn't have the same ring to it. Wouldn't you agree?" He looked to his cousin then only to find his face squeezed into an expression of concern.

"You're rather odd," Liam said softly. "Sometimes I forget, but sometimes it really shows."

Tuck smiled. "Someone must be the odd one in the family."

Liam held up a finger. "That title has already been claimed by Uncle Fitzwilliam."

Tuck's face fell. "I'm afraid you're right. It was quite fascinating when he took up taxidermy, but it was something else entirely when he started staging the taxidermied squirrels into famous scenes from operas."

"Agreed," Liam said, and that was it as Birdie entered their peripheral vision, a stream of women following her.

The beading along the woman's gown clicked as she approached, and Tuck couldn't help but think it reminiscent of the clicking heels of a general of Her Majesty's army. He straightened, a sense of foreboding washing over him as they drew near.

This was what his midnight lady had been talking about, this moment happening before him. Something was about to start for Liam, and Tuck was oddly queasy at being an accomplice to the first stirrings of the Marriage Mart.

Didn't anyone simply fall in love anymore?

Was it always to be like this, a matching of titles and

coffers? Each party weighed by the other for faults and commendations?

What had happened to love?

He pushed away his silly thoughts as Birdie stopped in front of them and began the formal introductions.

Lady Stoke Bruerne was the tall brunette with the pearls Tuck had noticed, and she brought with her a near replica, a lady perhaps only a handful of years younger than Tuck. He knew her to be the widow Liam had mentioned as she wore a plain gown of an indeterminate shade of purple. Lady Stoke Bruerne turned as if to introduce another daughter, but the space beside the widow was empty.

"I do beg your pardon," she said, her voice deeper than Tuck would have expected for a lady, but it almost rang with authority. She looked behind her, and although she hissed, Tuck heard it plainly. "Eloise!"

There was a muffled gasp of surprise, a good deal of shuffling, some not so muffled admonishing, and then Lady Stoke Bruerne straightened, a bright smile painted on her face as the youngest Stoke Bruerne daughter took her place beside the widow.

And that was the moment Tuck's entire world shattered.

Because standing before him, her face finally fully revealed to him in the light of a thousand candles was his magical midnight lady, the realization stopping his heart just as Birdie announced, "And this is Lady Eloise Bounds."

Eloise.

It wasn't Ellen, Ellie, or Elaine.

Horribly, it was Eloise.

CHAPTER 2

*N*o.

No, this wasn't happening or no, it couldn't be him. Either would have applied just then.

For a solitary moment as Lady Heyworth led them over to the gentlemen, her mind had played a devious trick on her, swapping the two so that for one terrible second she thought her midnight gentleman was the duke.

But it wasn't the duke. She knew that. It was only her fragile mind trying to escape the thing she had resigned herself to, trying one last feeble attempt to latch on to something that would save her.

Tuck.

He was the duke's cousin. That was what Lady Heyworth was saying. Her sister Annie was curtsying; their mother curtsied. Eloise couldn't remember how it was done, but her legs were suddenly moving, her head dipping.

The Honorable Mr. Tucker Ryan.

Not a duke at all.

"My cousin has graciously accepted my invitation to join

me in London for the season," Ardley was saying when Eloise's ears finally stopped ringing.

But although the duke was speaking, her eyes never left Tuck's. He had asked her to call him Tuck. How was she supposed to address him as Mr. Ryan now? Act as though they'd never met when, in fact, their meeting had been the greatest accident of her life?

"Oh, how lovely," Eloise's mother said, leaning forward on the word *lovely* as if this would help emphasize her meaning. "I do hope you'll find it to your liking, Mr. Ryan. Have you never been in town for a season before?"

Eloise forced her eyes to blink. She'd been staring for too long. What was wrong with her? The duke was going to think there was something odd about her, and the entire season would be a failure before it had hardly begun.

Not an entire failure. She couldn't think that because just that morning in a startling turn of events, her oldest sister, Gwendolyn, had left for Yorkshire to marry a sheep farmer. Gwen, the one sister Eloise had counted on to remain on the shelf, the one she was sure would not have a stake in this season's duel over the dukes.

Gwen had gotten herself a husband.

It wasn't a love match. It wasn't close to as much. Gwen hadn't even met her future husband, and she wouldn't until she landed on his doorstep in Yorkshire.

Still. It stung.

Gwen had a match. Gwen was finished with all this business of matchmaking. Gwen was going to be a wife.

Something twisted in Eloise's chest, and she hated herself for her sudden jealousy over her sister's situation. After all, Gwen could be walking into a nightmare, hitching herself forever to a boar of a man that smelled of moldy cheese and three-day-old ale.

Tuck didn't smell like moldy cheese. He smelled like the

pine of the firs that marked the path in the courtyard upon which she'd discovered him. She had thought him a wood nymph, something sprung from a fairy tale and partly a result of her overactive imagination.

But he wasn't. He was real, and he was standing in front of her, and they were forced to pretend they had never met before that very minute.

"No," Tuck said then, answering Eloise's mother, yet his gaze never left hers. "I'm finding it rather...extraordinary."

The word zinged through her like a flurry of bubbles traveling through every one of her veins.

Extraordinary.

What a deliberate word. Had he chosen that for her? Was *she* extraordinary?

Oh God, she couldn't be. She just *couldn't.*

It took an effort she would never have believed she possessed to wrench her gaze from his and fix it on the duke. She was staring at him for a full three seconds when she registered the quizzical look on his face as he returned her gaze.

Oh heavens, what was her face doing? What expression was she giving? She didn't know. She couldn't even *feel* her face any longer.

She forced her shoulders back and raised her chin.

Eloise Cassandra Bounds was trained for precisely this moment, and she would not allow one starry night to sweep her off her feet.

Then why was her attention skittering back to Tuck? Why was she listening so intently while her mother questioned him?

"You come from Derbyshire then?" Eloise's mother asked.

Tuck nodded. "Originally, yes. Most recently I find myself in Oxford. I have a lecturer position there, and I've been conducting research into the aurora borealis."

The northern lights.

Her attention was fully on him again, but she allowed it this time. She'd read of the aurora borealis in her father's scientific journals, the ones he procured because it looked good on his part but which he never read. She liked the illustrations, the whimsy and magic of them. To think somewhere in the world such light displays existed naturally.

"What kind of research are you conducting?" The question was out before she knew she would ask it.

This would never do. She couldn't possibly be seen to exhibit *interest* in the man. No, she couldn't. But then she noticed the duke's expression had turned calculating.

He was watching her, studying her, *assessing* her.

Come, Eloise, she chided herself, *now is the time to act.*

And act she did. She tilted her head just so as she had practiced in the mirror to look intrigued but not curious. Curiosity was not a desirable trait in a wife.

"I endeavor to launch an expedition to Spitsbergen, an archipelago in the Arctic Ocean where I'll be able to study the aurora borealis firsthand."

"Spitsbergen." She whispered the word while her mind raced through the various illustrations she'd studied of the far-flung locale in her father's journals. "I've heard Spitsbergen is cruelly cold but beautiful."

Tuck nodded, but his eyes narrowed cautiously. "Beautiful but extreme, I would say. It's no place for a holiday of leisure. Temperatures can dip dangerously low in the winter, and the archipelago is home to polar bears. One must exercise the utmost caution and wherewithal should one attempt an expedition in the territory."

"Have you been there then?" she asked, aware her voice had gone breathless again.

The light in his eyes dimmed. "No, I'm afraid I haven't."

There was such heartache in his voice that it tugged at

her, almost pulling her toward him. She felt herself tipping, yearning to soothe him, wishing to bolster his dreams, support him in any way she could.

But there was no way.

Only if she were his wife could she give him such comfort, but her station as a debutante kept her isolated.

"I know you'll make it there one day," she said, forcing cheer into her voice before resolutely turning her gaze to the duke. "It's so kind of you to host your cousin this season, Your Grace." The words sounded artificial, and she hoped the gaiety of the room and the ever-flowing champagne made it less obvious.

Ardley smiled, and she realized there was true warmth there. "It is the least I can do for not only my cousin but my one true friend."

While her own words had lacked authenticity, Ardley was sincere, and it jolted her. The duke was…*nice*. She wasn't sure what she had been anticipating, but likely her resistance to this entire endeavor had led her to presume the duke would be another stuffy aristocrat, like all the others she had encountered in her two seasons out.

But with this realization came another. It made it so much worse that she should covet this man's cousin while actively attempting to win his proposal.

Oh Lord, she was a harlot.

Heat flooded her face, and she only hoped it did not appear in pink blotches on her cheeks. "You are close then?" she asked, and the jab of her mother's elbow into her side was swift and sharp.

Her mother's admonishment was justified. The question was terribly personal, but she couldn't help it. The sudden appearance of her shadowy gentleman had thrown her, and it was all she could do to place words in the correct order to form a sentence.

Ardley threw his arm around Tuck, his smile broadening. "Thick as thieves, as they say."

Tuck's smile was sheepish. His gaze fell to the floor as his cousin embraced him, and she wondered if he weren't used to such affection or was it merely that he was unused to such demonstration in public. Whichever it was, the sight of them tugged at her. This man was nothing if not mercurial. From the excitement he'd exhibited in showing her his modified railroad glasses to the bashful display before her and most intriguing of all, the quiet strength he exuded, the very strength she had felt when he'd pressed himself to her back, the man was as mysterious as his northern lights.

But then he raised his eyes, and unerringly, his gaze found hers, and for one horrible moment, they were locked there, seeing only each other, and in that infinite second, their future rolled out before her.

Eloise and Tuck, husband and wife. She would support him, helping him with his endeavor in any way possible. She would even follow him to Spitsbergen if that was what it took to see his dream of this expedition fulfilled. It was all she had ever wanted, to be a wife, a helpmate, a mother. It sounded terribly old-fashioned, but maybe she was old-fashioned. There was something so peacefully alluring in the idea of creating something, building a family, and watching it grow just like her parents had done.

Perhaps she would even enjoy some adventure in the process. She hadn't thought of it. It hadn't been an option before that moment, and she'd never considered it. But to be free of those watercolors and needlepoint? To experience something…more?

Here it was standing before her, all that she had ever dreamed of, but it was too late. It was time for her to set aside her childish dreams of love. Two seasons' worth of her mother's admonishments had taught her it was past time for Eloise Bounds to grow up.

So she would.

Once more she wrenched her gaze from Tuck and smiled at the duke. The smile came more easily now, but it came with a price, that of her heart slowly breaking.

"You're incredibly lucky to have one another then," she said, and the light in Ardley's eyes changed, and it felt as though she'd passed some test.

Relief flooded her, swift as lightning, and she drew the first deep breath since coming into conversation with the duke and his cousin. She *could* do this. If Gwen could travel to Yorkshire to marry a man she'd never met, Eloise could be the debutante she was trained to be for the Duke of Ardley, even if it meant her heart was somewhere else, saving itself for some*one* else.

She curled her toes in her slippers, grounding herself there in the ballroom of what was going to be the first of many social obligations which she would attend to win the Duke of Ardley's proposal.

When she was finally feeling steady once more, the duke himself not only pulled the rug out from beneath her, but he rolled it up and tossed it onto a bonfire.

"I'm glad you think so, Lady Eloise, for I think my cousin would very much enjoy a dance with you."

"What?" The word shot from her lips like a social death sentence.

Her mother's elbow to her ribs then was more lethal than a dagger, and she thought she might just die and be prevented from having to dance with the man who had stolen her heart under the watchful eye of the moon.

But if she were to expire of social death, Tuck looked as if he had just been told he would eat eel for the remainder of his life. The color drained from his face, and his lips parted wordlessly.

"Yes, a dance is in order, I should think," Ardley was saying, but it was only noise in her ears as she tried to interpret the expression on Tuck's face, the rampaging beat of her own heart, and the tingling in her fingertips as if she'd just snuffed a flame with her bare hands.

Her mother was making an agreeable noise—agreeable!—and the duke had turned to whisper something in his cousin's ear, but it was so quick, she might have misunderstood because then Tuck was nodding, his arm extending, and then—

She wished for once in her life to be one of those debutantes who was skilled at fainting dead away, but she was not.

So instead she danced with the Honorable Mr. Tucker Ryan.

* * *

HE COULDN'T TELL Liam why this was a very bad idea.

Even with his cousin's words reverberating in his ear, further evidence of why dancing with Eloise was the worst possible thing he could do in that moment, Tuck still couldn't admit as to why.

Because if he did, Eloise would be ruined.

A midnight encounter in a secluded courtyard?

She'd be ruined for sure.

Oh God, he must stop thinking of her as Eloise. She was Lady Eloise, daughter of the Earl Stoke Bruerne, someone deserving of his respect. Someone entirely perfect for his cousin, the Duke of Ardley.

He glanced at Liam to find the man smiling idiotically, his

head giving the smallest of nods as if to remind Tuck of his assignment.

Did his cousin truly wish for Tuck to assess Lady Eloise and give Liam his opinion on her as a potential wife?

Tuck would rather lose a toe to hypothermia.

Instead he smiled, graciously, and offered his arm to the lady as protocol required. The orchestra played the opening chords to a quadrille, and he thanked whatever deity that might be listening that it wasn't a waltz. A quadrille was easy. In fact, he'd hardly even be forced to speak to Eloise, let alone touch her.

Oh God. Touch her.

Lady Eloise.

Lady Eloise.

Lady. Eloise.

He was doomed.

But then Liam caught his arm, pulled him back just enough to whisper further damning instructions into his ear. "Promenade with her after this dance, won't you? You'll hardly have a chance to speak to her otherwise."

Tuck wanted to run from the room, maybe from London entirely, but instead he gave that same gracious smile and turned them onto the dance floor.

He let go of her as soon as he could, stepping into the line to begin the dance. When he finally allowed himself to look at her face, he found her expression hovering between stark naked fear and resignation. At least they shared similar feelings on the matter.

He had looked away, glancing down the line of assembled dancers before her expression finally registered, and he looked back at her. Only this time she was watching him, and their eyes met, and the rest of the world fell away.

Because when he had seen her terrified expression, he

had only registered that her feelings were likely the same as his, but he hadn't registered what that meant.

That she felt the same way about him as he felt about her.

The ballroom vanished, the chatter and the music dying away, until there was only the thumping of his heart, the soft whooshing of the blood traveling through his veins, and... her.

He could see it now, from the light of a thousand candles above them, the hope and terror and—Oh God, *longing*—in her eyes as her gaze remained steady on his, unable to look away just as he was unable to do so.

How was it possible? How could he know between the beats of his beleaguered heart that she was everything he had ever wanted?

No. No. No.

This couldn't be happening. Not now. Not like this. She was meant for Liam, not for him. He couldn't have her. He was only here to find a benefactor, and she was—

Everything.

She glowed in the candlelight, and it was a moment before he realized he had the luxury of seeing her now, her features and coloring revealed like it hadn't been in the moonlight. Her dark golden hair was pulled back from a face that seemed to radiate the light of a thousand stars, her eyes reflecting deep brown warmth, and her mouth—well, it was perfect. Perfect for smiling, perfect for laughing, perfect for—

Someone jostled his shoulder, and he realized the music had started, the dancers were moving, and they had been lost in their own stargazing. His feet remembered the steps even when he did not, and soon they were sweeping across the dance floor, his ears filled with notes he didn't hear. He tripped more than once when his gaze moved to follow her instead of the twirling dancers, and when the dance brought them back together again, he never wished to let go of her.

But he must as the steps of the dance separated them, and she was once more swept away.

How excruciatingly long was this dance?

It seemed to go on forever, and he was forced to keep his focus on the steps lest he trample an innocent debutante. But more than that, he must keep up appearances. He mustn't let on what was happening. For anything, even so minor as a glance two seconds too long, would be sniffed out by the first matron, and Eloise's reputation would be ruined. The scandal would be immense. Tuck was the cousin of the duke pursuing the young lady after all. He could not imagine a juicier morsel for the *ton* to devour.

The reel swung them about, bringing them together again. He took her hands, the steps dictating he move them in a quick succession of sidesteps. At least the swiftness of this series of steps required him to keep his gaze on their trajectory rather than her face.

Her beautiful, astounding, breathtaking—

"I think we have a problem, Mr. Ryan."

Eloise's voice was little more than a whisper, but it was as though a gong erupted in his ear. His eyes flew to hers, and he nearly toppled them over a baron. He swung them about, completing the same series of steps in the direction from which they had just come.

"I would agree, Lady Eloise," he whispered back. "But what are we to do of it?"

She shook her head so quickly he wouldn't have noticed if he weren't hanging on to her, but then the dance separated them once more. He accepted the hand of another partner, twirling her about in time with the reel until he found himself once more standing beside Eloise, the dance finished.

He couldn't look at her. He didn't dare. Everyone would know.

He held out his arm, and she took it, and he couldn't understand how no one knew right then. Couldn't they see it? This inferno that had inexplicably ignited between them? An inferno that could have only been started by a lightning strike, unstoppable and unpredictable.

He moved to the side of the dance floor, his pace sedate, their progress slow as they wound their way through the dancers. A few of the debutantes who had been partnered with other gentlemen in the quadrille exchanged pleasantries with Eloise, but their words were foreign sounding in his ears, and they may have well been speaking in gibberish for all he understood.

His heart was going to erupt from his chest, and he would die directly on the dance floor. Something must be done.

Her grip on his arm tightened, and he realized she was pulling him away from the crowd to the periphery of the room where refreshment tables were set up, and matrons and wallflowers lingered. Did she hope to slip amongst them? Get lost in the mundane of it all?

But no, she was pulling him *through* the matrons and wallflowers, past the refreshment tables, and to the corridor beyond. They were leaving the ballroom.

His feet cemented themselves to the floor without his knowing, and Eloise snapped backward like a plucked string. Her eyes rounded in disbelief and not a little bit of blame. She wasn't wrong. He was drawing attention to them, attention they didn't need, but if they left the ballroom, it would be all over. They would be alone again, and this time it would be so much worse because he knew who she was. She was forbidden, and forbidden things were always so much more tempting.

He tried to communicate with his eyes that he couldn't

take another step when she marched directly up to him, her voice strikingly low.

"I must speak to you, Mr. Ryan. We must sort this out. Do you wish to do this here where all of London can see us or would you prefer somewhere more private?"

She had a point. A very good one.

He forced his legs to move, pulling her arm more securely through his as they made their way to the corridor. The silence was jarring as they slipped through the archway into the dim light of the hallway beyond. What little sound carried through from the ballroom was muffled by the carpeted floor and the tapestries hanging thick on the walls. He tried to remember the name of the family whose home this was, but any of his thoughts before finding Eloise again were null, and his brain had simply swept them away. Whoever the family was who owned this house, their wealth was clearly old and stuffy judging by the weight of their furnishings.

Without preamble, Eloise opened one of the doors along the corridor and stuck her head inside. He jumped back as though a cobra would emerge from the crack between the doors. But only Eloise emerged, her face set.

"Come on," she hissed and stopped, surveying him. "What is it?"

He gestured to the door. "Someone could have been in there."

Her frown was swift. "And I would have told them I was looking for the retiring room."

His expression fell. Yet another good point she made.

He gestured to the door, all but shoving her inside the room. He gave one last look along the corridor to ensure they hadn't been seen before slipping into the room behind her. He wanted to slam the door shut as if they would keep out the threat of discovery, the reality of what he was doing there, the betrayal he was about to commit.

Betrayal.

The word sliced through him, and he bit down on his cheek as he turned about to find Eloise standing just behind him, her hands clenched together in front of her.

"This isn't as bad as it would seem."

Oh God, she was even more beautiful in this room. In—

He swept his gaze quickly around the room, assessing it for hiding spots. He pressed a single finger to his lips as he strode across the room and assaulted the curtains that hung at the windows there. Finding them free of spies who would report him to Liam, he checked the space under the desk next and even the minuscule space below the two sofas. It was all empty. They were alone.

"It isn't?" he said, standing up from his crouch along the floor and brushing the dust from his hands and the knees of his trousers. "We're alone in a—" He paused, looked around again. "Is this a drawing room?"

Eloise followed his gaze. "It looks like such. Probably the family drawing room too. Look at those newspapers."

Her hand gestured to a haphazard stack of newspapers strewn about a low table beside one of the sofas. There was an ashtray on the table by a chair in the corner, a clay pipe forgotten along its brim. Two teacups were discarded on the desk, and there was even a handkerchief slumbering beneath a pile of magazines. If it wasn't the family's drawing room, the staff required some remediation on how to properly keep a room.

He turned back to Eloise, but she hadn't moved from her place by the door, and he was struck again by the absurdity of the situation. His entire life was changing second by second, and he was surrounded by the clutter of a strange family's everyday life. It just wasn't possible.

He must focus. "We're alone again, Eloise." He stopped himself, pressed his fingers to each temple. "I must stop calling you that. Lady Eloise."

"Eloise is really fine."

He looked sharply at her and found her expression had softened. From stark fear it had melted to the wondering disbelief he had seen the night before in the courtyard. It pulled at him, like a magnet finding its match, and it was all he could do to resist it.

But maybe he didn't resist it because suddenly he was standing in front of her. His hands were lifting, his fingers finding the curve of her cheek, the one he had wanted to trace since laying eyes on her once more.

But he didn't touch her. He couldn't.

The inferno raged, and if he touched her, it would set off an explosion from which they could not come back.

"I can't call you Eloise." His voice had dropped, but he couldn't say why. "You're not mine to call you something so familiar."

Her tongue darted out, wetting her lower lip. "No, I'm not yours." Her voice was low too, and he wondered why.

"We haven't done anything that can't be undone." The words sounded strange even to his own ears, as if he were convincing himself of something instead of speaking to her.

She shook her head but only a little. "No, we haven't." There was a pause, a pause he felt as if it had stepped directly on his chest. And then— "Not yet."

The words rang through the air, but only for a second.

Because then he kissed her, and she kissed him, and everything else was forgotten.

CHAPTER 3

$\mathcal{N}$ever before had Eloise believed it when someone was said to be not of sound mind. She had always thought it an excuse for bad behavior. But right then she very much understood it. Because her mind had quite simply stood up and wandered off. It must have. For why else was she kissing the cousin of the man from whom she was supposed to be attempting to win a proposal?

Madness was the only answer. She simply had leave of her senses. Nothing else could have explained it.

This man, this Tucker Ryan, had woven some kind of magical spell over her. It had wound its way through her skin, tucking itself in between pores and behind cells until it was so much a part of her, she could never be separate from it again. But how had he done it?

Eloise had had her fair share of suitors over the two seasons she'd been out. She wasn't so modest as to pretend she wasn't pretty. While she wasn't beautiful, she knew her features held some appeal, but it was her personality she liked best. So while her prettiness drew suitors in, her charm was what had kept them there. This had resulted in a few shy kisses, perhaps an awkward exchange of affectionate words, but it had all been so playful and light.

This was nothing like that had been.

This was…this was…heavens, she didn't even know, and for that very reason, she knew it must be magic. Must be for how else could this near stranger have such a hold over her?

Why was she kissing him *back*?

Maybe it had been she who had kissed him. She didn't even know any longer or care. She stood on tiptoe, her arms winding their way around his neck to hold on to him, wanting every piece of herself to be pressed against every part of him. He seemed to want the same thing as his hands pressed into her back, his fingers kneading and exploring, taking and keeping.

And she gave, her lips tangling with his, her fingers delving into his thick hair—even his hair was magical—and she forgot for just a second to hate herself for what she was doing. Hate herself for this selfishness. She had sworn this season would be different. She had discarded her fanciful dreams of a love match. Two dukes were too many to ignore, and the reality of a woman's place in society was highlighted in stark relief.

Marry well or face a difficult life.

She knew that to be the truth, but instead she was ravishing a near stranger in another stranger's drawing room.

She wrenched away so abruptly their lips made a smacking sound as they disconnected. She fell backward, catching herself against one of the sofas before she tumbled to the floor. Pressing the back of one hand to her aching lips, she blinked, trying to right her vision.

Finally she took him in, standing where she had abandoned him. His hands hung in the air, and it was as if they still molded her body. Every one of her muscles reacted, tightening at the sight of his hands, registering how painfully his fingers curled. *Possessively.*

She swallowed. "I don't even know you," she managed. "I only met you last night. You...you..." She searched for something damning and flung out a hand when she found it. "You could hate kittens."

His hands didn't move as he replied, so terribly softly. "I love kittens. Especially calico ones."

"Of course, you'd love kittens," she spat. "Everyone loves kittens. You'd need to be a rampaging murderer to *not* love kittens." She eyed him. "You're not a rampaging murderer, are you?"

"Not that I'm aware of." His tone never changed, holding to the same steady soft cadence she was coming to expect from him. She wondered if he weren't as effected as she had been, but then she realized his hands still hung in the air where she had stood in his embrace.

"Coffee or tea?" The question burst from her. The need to find a difference she could drive between them urging her on.

"Coffee."

"Damn," she swore, her hand flying to her mouth in shock. What was this man doing to her? She flung out a hand again. "A promenade in the park or a dance at a ball?"

He wrinkled his nose. "Neither." He waited a beat as if searching, and then a light came into his eyes, a light that seemed to call to her. "Coasting. I'd prefer coasting, preferably at dusk with the moon rising on the horizon. There's nothing quite like coasting in the dark." He paused, considered. "As long as there's nothing you might crash into."

Her hand dropped of its own volition. "Coasting?"

He nodded, his own hands finally falling. "There was a

terrific hill for coasting where I grew up." He smiled then, a smile of such joy it pulled her from her stupor.

He was handsome but not in the traditional sense. His face was too full of light and playfulness for that. She'd mussed his tawny hair with her wandering fingers, but she had a feeling a lock always fell over his brow like that, adding to the boyishness of his face but with a more rakish bent.

"When I was eleven, I attempted to build a sledge of my own. I nearly cut off an arm when I made the runners too sharp." His voice trembled with a laugh, and she couldn't stop her smile from mirroring his. "Liam wouldn't even test it with me. Thought he would be decapitated if he hit a berm at the wrong angle."

His smile vanished and so did hers at the reminder of what, in fact, they were doing. *Who* they were betraying.

She backed way, her hands sliding along the edge of the sofa as if it were a lifeline, and she was forced to grope her way in the sudden darkness that had descended over her from the haze of lust she was now peering through.

"It was just a kiss," she clamored on.

"That's right," he was quick to agree. "Just a kiss. No one must ever know of it."

Well, that sounded terribly guilty. He seemed to think so as well because his brow furrowed, and his gaze dropped to the floor.

She'd made her way to the corner of the sofa by then and pushed herself around it, her hands going to the arm of the furniture so she was forced to bend nearly in half, but she just couldn't let go of it.

Because if she did she'd run right back to him, throw herself in his arms, and—

Make the worst mistake of her life.

That realization felt like an Arctic blast sweeping through

the drawing room, and suddenly she was able to let go of the sofa. She straightened, her arms falling uselessly at her sides.

It wasn't that pursuing this magical thing that had erupted between her and a near stranger was silly and futile; it was that it couldn't happen at all. She was destined to marry a duke that season. And likely, it would be this man's very cousin.

No, what was happening between them wasn't silly. It was impossible.

"Mr. Ryan, I—"

"Tuck."

The way he spoke his own name had her stopping. The single word was filled with sadness and longing and worst of all, acceptance. As if she could give him this one thing, calling him by his given name, when she could give him nothing else.

"Tuck." She spoke the name like the gift it was and then swallowed, prepared to sever whatever it was that had sprung up between them. "We can't do this. I'm supposed to marry your—" Her throat closed around the word *cousin*, and she felt the distinct prick of tears. She couldn't cry, not now, not over something so silly and so important. She forced a smile and straightened her shoulders. "I'm to marry a duke this season." Her voice was brittle with unshed tears, but she pretended instead it was a laugh. "My mother will settle for no less."

Tuck's smile was hesitant, and she thought it was likely in response to her show of bravado rather than any happy feelings.

"Whatever it is that is between us now is just a lark. An accident of our meeting. It will go away in a few days." Oh lud, was she speaking of love or a fever?

His smile faded. "You're right, Lady Eloise. We're nothing

but the victims of biology. There isn't anything more to it." His words sounded as false as hers had.

She forced another one of those smiles. "Then we are in agreement. This is nothing." The tears almost came then, and she felt like the silly little girl she'd been two years ago when she'd been thrust onto the Marriage Mart.

She had swept through her first ballroom with visions of romance and love and affection only to find her suitors measuring her like a prized mare, sizing her up for her wealth and connections and most importantly of all, her ability to bear children. There was nothing romantic about any of it, and love was as real as unicorns.

"It might be best if we were to avoid one another," he said.

The idea sliced through her like a dagger, and she thought she might never breathe again. Avoid each other? Not see him? It couldn't be and yet at the same time it must.

"You're right," she replied. "Perhaps if we were to see less of one another these feelings will grow stale and fade."

Liar.

She knew she spoke lies, but she must believe she was telling the truth. Too much depended on her making the proper match. Her mother would be so disappointed if she didn't secure the hand of the duke, and something deep inside of Eloise wouldn't let that happen. She needed to grow up, had *decided* to grow up and then—

She'd met Tuck.

It didn't matter. It *couldn't* matter. She'd already made her choice.

Besides, Ardley seemed like a fair gentleman. Perhaps her marriage wouldn't be without laughter or kindness. The very thought felt empty when she was looking at Tuck.

So she looked away, her feet moving her toward the door when her mind told her to stay, and her heart was already back in Tuck's arms.

"I'll leave first," she heard herself say. "We shouldn't be seen coming back into the ballroom together. There will be talk." She turned back at this to see if he understood.

She was surprised to find he'd buried his face in one hand. At her words, he straightened, sweeping the hand up his face until it pushed through his hair, spiking the lock that fell over his forehead backward and up, entirely ruining any style he might have meant to make of it earlier that evening. But when the lock fell back into place as if he hadn't made that gesture, she wondered if he'd attempted a style at all. Maybe this was just him, that wayward lock and that gesture of frustration.

It was one of the millions of little things about him she'd never learn.

"You're right, of course," he said. "I shall wait here for a time."

She nodded. "Thank you, Tuck. I'm—" She had almost said she was sorry, but she wasn't sorry. She could never be sorry about Tucker Ryan. She could only be sorry that she'd met him too late. "I'm lucky to have met you at all," she said instead and then forced another smile as she slipped through the door.

She didn't go back to the ballroom. She found a retiring room down the empty corridor and locked herself inside of it. When she finished crying, she scolded herself for her immaturity and gave herself the talking to she deserved.

It was only infatuation she felt for Tucker Ryan, and it would fade. It must.

She fixed her hair, smoothed her skirts, and when she let herself out of the retiring room, she promised one day she'd believe such an idea might be true.

* * *

STANDING in a crowded drawing room surrounded by enough starched cravats to hold up Big Ben, Tucker Ryan was fairly certain it was the worst day of his life.

He'd once spent seven days on a ship anchored off of the Shetland Islands, assisting his mentor, a Professor Ludgate, in studying a colony of puffins. A storm raged over the island for five of those seven days, pounding the researchers with fifty-mile-an-hour winds, lashing, unrelenting rain, and eight-foot swells. Even the heartiest of sailors on board their vessel became ill with seasickness, but the storm prevented them from going ashore or even taking the chance of finding a harbor. The coastline was too rocky, and the inclement weather meant death to all of them if it lifted their ship against the dangerous rocks.

So instead, they remained at sea, weathering the storm, and the seasickness that plagued them. By the third day, the stench of sick had been burned into Tuck's nostrils, and he was certain he'd die from sleep deprivation. Even then, Tuck had felt more at home than he did standing on the edges of that drawing room on a dismal Tuesday afternoon in Mayfair.

Liam had said it was important for Tuck to mingle in a setting that was less demanding than a ball. He thought calling on one of Liam's prospective wives would be a casual affair and give Tuck the chance to make some new acquaintances.

So here Tuck stood, a cup of tea gone cold in his hand as he lazily spun the floor-standing globe at his elbow, seeing where his finger might land and if he were familiar with the location when it did.

The debutante Liam had decided to call on was a Lady Frances Hipplewaite, the daughter of the Earl of Leighton. She was a nice enough girl, although girl was truly the description for her. Liam had said she was only seven and ten, rather young to be out already, and Tuck felt bad that she had been forced to give up the innocence and ease of childhood so quickly. She had a nice smile in an unfortunate face, and he wondered if she would find criticism amongst the ladies of the *ton* now that she was out. Wallflower was the word Tuck thought might be used to describe her, and it seemed a shame.

But her drawing room was filled to the rafters that afternoon, evidence of the sizable dowry her father had bestowed upon her. Perhaps he too was aware of his daughter's inevitable wallflower status.

Tuck should be speaking to someone, anyone, really. He wished to embark on his journey by that August, so that he would be fully established in Spitsbergen before the aurora borealis returned in the fall. There was much to be done before then, and without funding, he could do none of it. Yet here he was twirling a globe instead of speaking to anyone.

Twirling a globe and trying not to think about Lady Eloise Bounds.

Why on earth had he kissed her?

When he'd returned to Liam, he'd claimed a headache and said he'd speak to his cousin in the morning, hurrying off before his cousin could probe further and discover the horrible thing Tuck had done.

Betrayal.

The word reverberated in his head like a curse, and there was nothing he could do to break it. He must remind himself that Lady Eloise was just one of Liam's prospects, and it wasn't as though his cousin had declared his undying love for the woman. He was merely interested in her as a potential wife.

God, Tuck was a failure.

This thought had his finger poking the globe harder than he should have, and it made a screeching noise against his flesh. He looked up, but nobody about him seemed to have noticed.

His view was mostly the backs of gentlemen waiting their turn to speak with Lady Frances, and most were involved in discussions of gambling and horseflesh, oblivious to the machinations of a bored scholar behind them.

Harrison wouldn't be bored. Harrison likely would have raised all the necessary funds already, acquired seven new friends, and pledged allegiance to a fraternity or six. Tuck gulped his tea, shoving thoughts of his brother down into the bottom of his gut where he preferred to let them fester.

It was then someone jostled his elbow, sending tea splashing down his shirtfront. He wiped lazily at it, certain no one would notice, and made to smile at the gentleman who had knocked into him to indicate no harm was done. Only when the gentleman turned about, he greeted Tuck with a kind smile and a soft expression of sympathetic misery.

"Apologies, my good man." The gentleman had a deeper voice than his lithe build would have suggested, a resounding baritone that cut through the din of conversation that surrounded them. "It's rather more…" His voice trailed off as he looked around the room as if deciding what word would best fit what he wished to say.

"Congested," Tuck offered, and this brought the gentleman's gaze back to him, the corners of his lips lifted in surprised mirth.

"Congested. Yes," he said. "That's quite the right word for it, I should think." He offered his hand. "The name is Templeton."

"Tucker Ryan," Tuck said, taking the man's hand.

"Are you here to vie for the affections of Lady Frances then?"

Tuck shook his head. "No, I'm afraid I'm merely accompanying my cousin." He nodded to where Liam occupied the sofa next to Lady Frances, her hand in his as he no doubt cooed epithets of undying love to her while a bevy of displeased suitors glared on around them. "The Duke of Ardley."

Templeton's expression fell. "So you're not here for Lady Frances then?"

"No, I'm afraid I'm not in the market for a wife. I'm only in London to raise funds for a scientific expedition I am hoping to launch this summer. Are you familiar with the northern lights?" He indicated the ceiling with a single finger, painting the aurora borealis as Michelangelo may have painted the ceiling of the Sistine Chapel. "The light phenomenon that is often witnessed in northerly skies?"

Templeton's expression slid downward into something resembling confusion, so Tuck went on, feeling the familiar excitement when it came to discussing the aurora.

"You see, the aurora borealis occurs when there is some kind of anomaly to the geomagnetic field. I'm sure you remember the Carrington Event. That was caused by these disturbances that manifest as light patterns in the sky. Not much is known on what causes these disturbances or why they had such an impact on the operations of human life, and it is this which I hope to study in my expedition."

Templeton looked as though he'd just eaten paste. "I'm sorry, Mr. Ryan. I must have given the wrong impression. I'm only a vicar." He nodded in the direction of Lady Frances. "The young lady's mother asked for me to be in attendance today to interview her daughter's possible suitors. She wishes for her daughter to wed a devoted Christian man."

Tuck realized he was still pointing at the ceiling then and slowly lowered his arm, tucking it against his body and hoping the floor would drop out from beneath him, allowing him to disappear entirely.

"I see," he muttered. "Well then, how goes the interviewing?"

Templeton's expression held notes of concern and empathy but mostly just the desire to be as far away from Tuck as possible. Tuck knew this because he was often looked at with such an expression.

He swallowed and stepped back. "You can leave," he said, gesturing to the rest of the room.

"Thank you," the vicar said and scuttled away.

"You scared off another one, didn't you?"

Tuck didn't even start at the sound of his cousin's voice so near his ear. He took another sip of his cold tea and grimaced at the bitterness. "I didn't scare him away. I only misunderstood the situation." He glanced at his cousin whose expression was inscrutable. "Again," Tuck added.

Liam rolled his eyes and shook his head slightly. "Tucker, my dear cousin, you must let me help. You know I applaud your abilities in the classroom, and I would never think to undermine your integrity as a researcher. But you're in my classroom now, and you must let me show you how it is one deals with society." He lifted his hand palm up to gesture about the room. "Follow me about, won't you?" His hand stopped at about eleven o'clock to indicate a pair of men wearing similar plaid trousers and peach waistcoats. "The Devlin brothers. Younger sons of a marquess. Educated at Oxford. Both with courtesy titles and allowances to see them through anything and both riddled with the pox they acquired at Mrs. Heathcliffe's House of Leisure." Liam dropped his hand and turned back to Tuck. "Offer them a chair and watch them squirm. I haven't seen them sit at a social function in three seasons. Their feats in the brothels are legendary. You would think they would wish a respite from the venereal pain, but they continue in their debauchery."

Tuck blinked. "How do you know about the sexual exploits of those gentlemen?"

"Because one must know. Such tidbits are the ammunition one must have to succeed in this town." His hand moved again, but Tuck couldn't look. "Lord Byram, staunch supporter of the Judicature Acts, and yet he's terrified of his own wife. He fakes migraines to avoid her." The hand moved again. "The Honorable Martin Wycliffe. Thrown from a horse so many times, the man even refuses to ride in a carriage. Will walk miles to avoid it." His hand dropped, and Tuck hoped fervently his cousin was finished. "You must discover more about who it is you wish to solicit before attempting to do so. Were you even aware Templeton was a vicar?"

Tuck opened his mouth, shut it, and shook his head instead.

"Did you think to ask him his name?"

"Ah," Tuck said, happy to have a point in his favor. "The gentleman offered his name as simply Templeton. I didn't know to ask more."

"You must let me help." Liam's expression was stern, but Tuck waved him off.

"I must persuade a gentleman of means to be my benefactor, not seduce him into bed."

Liam pressed a hand to his chest in mock indignation. "I am not a rogue, cousin. I am merely a man who appreciates the finer things this life has to offer."

"The finer things being women."

"Ladies," Liam corrected. "Please, Tucker. Do not offend me with your baser accusations."

His cousin grew quiet then, his eyes no longer playful. Tuck shifted, setting aside the teacup he'd nearly forgotten. He didn't like it when Liam grew thoughtful. His cousin knew him better than anyone, which only meant he knew the sorest places to poke.

"Have you given any more thought as to what I said?" Liam finally asked, his voice soft. "About approaching potential funders with *why* you are doing this instead of the science of the thing?"

Tuck suddenly wished for another cup of tea, or perhaps something stronger, as his throat grew scratchy at his cousin's words. He shook his head.

"You know I will not pursue such a line of inquiry. It is no concern of my potential benefactors why it is I've set my sights on this expedition. The merits of science should be enough to win their dollars."

"And how was it that the vicar felt about the aurora?"

Tuck only frowned.

"Precisely. You must give these men something they can relate to, or you'll just find yourself watching their backsides as they walk away from you."

Tuck felt that familiar sensation of falling, the one he had felt for so many years now, ever since the stranger had shown up on their doorstep with the news that would set the course of his life.

He faced his cousin. "I will not speak of Harrison. These people don't deserve to know of him or what happened to him. This is about the expedition and the science that can be gained from it. That is all."

Liam's expression held a degree of empathy that always made Tuck feel instantly guilty for rebuffing his cousin's attempt at aid. He dropped his gaze and forced a breath out of his lungs before looking up.

"I'm not ready, Liam. Not yet."

"It's been fourteen years, cousin. When will you be ready?" Liam questioned delicately.

Tuck couldn't answer.

His cousin shifted and blew out a breath. "Did you ever think you'd have an easier go at this if you could speak of him?"

The question dug into Tuck's chest like an arrow, sapping the breath from his lungs as he'd never considered the question.

"I guess we'll never find out," Tuck answered because he knew the truth of it.

He simply couldn't talk about his dead brother.

CHAPTER 4

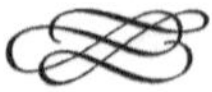

$\mathcal{E}$loise pondered how soon was too soon to visit her sister Gwen in Yorkshire.

Her sister was, after all, newly wed. Did that mean a certain period of time was required to allow the newlyweds some peace to settle in and begin to know one another? Or was that precisely the point?

No one except Father knew this Yorkshire sheep farmer. He could be a horrible man, and poor Gwen was left alone with him. Eloise would be saving her from a torturous existence if only she were to visit her sister all the way up north in Yorkshire.

Or Eloise was simply trying to find a way to run from the mess she'd made of her life.

That was probably more like it.

She slouched in her seat, not caring if she wrinkled her gown. They were once more at the modiste, and her mother and Annie were once again engaged in their favorite argument. Whether or not lilac was too bold a color for Annie's half-mourning.

Technically Annie was free from the strictly required

period of mourning, but for whatever reason had chosen to wear half-mourning colors this season. It really was a pity. Annie's coloring so favored bolder colors, and Eloise thought it a loss to see her sister in such drab as grays and lavenders.

"I don't know why we're wasting our time here," Grandmother Bitsy proclaimed from the chair next to Eloise's.

Eloise glanced over at her grandmother who poked through a plate of eclairs as though none of them suited her. She pushed aside a particularly squished one and daintily extracted one with a slick of chocolate frosting. She sniffed it and returned it to the plate.

"How's that, Grandmother?" Eloise asked when it was clear her grandmother had lost track of the conversation.

"Annie," she said, gesturing with another eclair, this one oozing cream from one end. "Poor Nancy shouldn't be wasting her time on fabrics like that. Annie will be wed to Grimsby before the end of the month. Mark my words."

Eloise sat up at this. "Grimsby?"

Gabriel Phelps, the Duke of Grimsby, was Annie's deceased husband's friend and confidante. The duke was a good man as far as Eloise knew. He had been kind to Annie in the days after her husband had died in a terrible accident, even going so far as to quell any gossip that may have resulted from the incident. For, in truth, Annie's husband had died during an unsanctioned boxing match in a gentlemen's club. Such a thing would have caused an uproarious scandal, but Grimsby had worked to conceal the truth of the matter, and the *ton* believed Wexford had died in a simple fall from his horse.

Eloise eyed her sister now as she pulled out a length of a particularly garish fabric in some color resembling smashed grapes.

"Has Annie indicated she might be receptive to such a proposal?" Eloise asked.

She and her sister were close, but Annie had been rather quiet since becoming a widow. They all assumed she was grieving, and Eloise, like the rest of the family, had given Annie leave to do so in peace. The result of that had meant Eloise and Annie hadn't spoken on such delicate matters in quite some time.

"It isn't Annie that I'm interested in," Grandmother Bitsy said, popping a bite of eclair into her mouth.

Eloise turned her gaze back to her grandmother. "Do you think Grimsby is the interested party?"

Grandmother Bitsy waggled her eyebrows. "Of course he is, dear. Have you seen the way the man looks at her?" She raised a single finger that was bent at the tip from arthritis. "Mark my words, dear. There are not two dukes on the Marriage Mart this season as everyone claims." She leveled that finger at Annie. "Because one of them is already smitten with our dear Annie."

Eloise narrowed her eyes. "How do you know that?"

Grandmother Bitsy dropped her hand. "I'm old," she said much too loudly. "I know things." She shrugged and went back to her eclairs.

Eloise watched her until Annie appeared between them, sweat on her brow and a lovely flush at her cheeks that finally brought some color to her face, but Eloise was too familiar with the cause of such a fluster and rose quickly.

"You must ignore Mother," she said, taking Annie's hands into her own. "She means well, you know? It's only she wishes to see us all make good matches, and she's worried about you."

Annie shook her head, and Eloise got the odd feeling her sister was close to tears. Eloise would speak to their mother about this. Annie was simply not ready to reenter society. She still grieved her husband deeply and needed time to—

Annie's expression had morphed from one of aggrieved

frustration to one of concerned curiosity, and Eloise followed the line of her gaze to find Grandmother Bitsy had stuck a finger into the end of an eclair only to pluck it out and suck the cream from the end of the digit. Her grandmother shook her head, disgust on her features, and put the eclair back on the plate.

Eloise turned back to Annie. "Let me speak with Mother. I'll help her to understand you need more time." She squeezed her sister's hands before making her way over to her mother who had moved on to a wall of pastels.

"Mother," Eloise began, but Nancy Bounds, Countess Stoke Bruerne, was not one to be easily swayed from her trajectory.

She spun about and held up a chiffon in buttery yellow. "What do you think of this? Wouldn't it look splendid with your sister's dark hair? I think I shall ask the modiste what she might do with this. Annie will love it."

Eloise reached out a hand and stopped her mother from continuing. "Mother. You must stop. Annie doesn't wish to leave her half-mourning."

Nancy dropped her hands, crumpling the chiffon in her annoyance. "She must leave her half-mourning. If the dukes are to—"

"Mother," Eloise said more sternly. "Annie is a *widow*. She's lost her husband. It's not like tearing a hem. She needs more time."

Her mother's eyes skittered over Eloise's shoulder to where Annie likely still stood next to Grandmother Bitsy. "But I want her to marry," Nancy nearly whined.

"We all do, Mother, but we must be patient. Weren't you always the one to tell me to hold my tongue when someone spoke ill of Gwen?"

Nancy's eyes came back to her, memory registering in her gaze. Gwen had suffered smallpox when she was only eight years old, and the ravaging disease had left its scars on her, scars the *ton* were only too gleeful in pointing out. There were many times her mother was forced to stop Eloise from engaging in a physical altercation to stop the other girls from snickering about Gwen.

"That was entirely different. Girls do not fight."

Eloise crossed her arms. "If they speak poorly about my sister, you'd best believe girls will fight."

Nancy's frown was swift and fierce. "You're right. I should marry you off first. You're far more trouble than Annie has ever been."

Eloise dropped her arms, alarm spiking through her at the realization she'd inadvertently drawn the conversation around to herself and her own prospects on a match.

"I promise I am taking all the necessary steps in catching the eye of the Duke of Ardley, Mother. You mustn't—"

"Oh, I know you are, child." Nancy replaced the chiffon on the rack with the rest of the yards of fabric with a casual flick as icy cold spread down Eloise's arms.

"You know?"

Nancy turned a blinding smile on her youngest daughter. "Oh yes," she said as if she'd been handed the Crown Jewels. "Ardley has asked your father for permission to court you. He'd like to take you promenading tomorrow in the park."

Eloise would have swallowed if any of the muscles in her body continued to work. "Tomorrow? Promenade?"

Nancy frowned, a line appearing between her brows. "Yes, promenading. You know the practice. Where parties interested in one another as a possible—"

Eloise cut off her mother. "I'm aware of what promenading is. I wasn't aware Ardley had expressed such interest."

Nancy's smile returned, possibly even more blinding than before. "Oh, he certainly has." She went back to scanning the fabrics before her. "Now do you think Madame Modiste will have time to fashion a new walking gown for you by tomorrow? We'll want you looking your best."

Tomorrow.

A hollow pit formed in her stomach, and she wondered if she could crawl inside of it and disappear. Because when she thought of Ardley, her terrible brain wondered if Tuck would be there too.

No. She mustn't think like that. They had agreed to stay as far away from each other as possible. Tuck mustn't accompany Ardley. He was likely busy securing that funding he was seeking. He didn't have time for Eloise, and he *shouldn't* have time for her. Oh drat, this was all a mess.

Was it too late to leave for Yorkshire? Perhaps she could sneak out in the morning before the house was awake.

"The weather has been fine for days now. We must hope it holds out for tomorrow." Nancy had moved to another line of fabrics. "Do you have that parasol your grandmother brought you back from Paris the last she was there?"

Parasol? What was her mother talking about?

"Mother," Eloise interjected, attempting to follow the woman through her inspection of fabrics. "Perhaps tomorrow isn't such a good time for a promenade. It's so early in the season. Do we wish to indicate to other suitors that I'm already spoken for? Ardley might not be inclined to act if he thinks he has me all to himself."

Her mother stopped her perusal, her hand frozen on a peach silk. She turned, ever so slowly, and when Eloise saw the calculating look in her mother's eye, the pit in her stomach turned into a sink hole.

"Oh Eloise, you're right." Her mother let go of the peach silk. "If we're to let on our eagerness for a match between you and the duke, he may believe he has all the time in the world to make his proposal." She set her hands to her hips. "We must not give him such a notion." Nancy stepped forward, her hand held out in Annie's direction. Eloise glanced behind her to see Annie attempting to keep Grandmother Bitsy from sampling every eclair on the plate. "Annie will go with you. If you are both seen with the duke, it will stir enough confusion for others to think you're not off the market completely. And what good that will be for Annie." Nancy brought her hands together in delight, and Eloise felt the pit in her stomach lessen.

Should the idea of being alone with the duke be so terrible? She must remember her goal in all of this. She would be married to the man after all. The idea of being in his presence shouldn't cause her such dread.

If only she hadn't kissed Tuck.

She forced a smile and nodded. She must make herself be positive about this. This could be her last season to make a match with someone as lofty as the duke. She couldn't fail, not now. Her mother would be so disappointed.

"That's a wonderful idea," she heard herself say, and her mother nodded in agreement, that wicked smile back on her face.

"Oh, I'm glad you think so." She turned back to the silks. "You know, we should ask Ardley to bring that cousin of his. That would be lovely, wouldn't it?" Nancy glanced over her shoulder. "It would give Annie someone to practice with. You know it's been so long since she's been out, and that Mr. Ryan fellow seemed so kind. He's just the thing for Annie to get her feet wet again."

Eloise could do nothing but stare and hope her heart didn't pound itself directly out of her chest.

* * *

"I don't know why I must accompany you."

Tuck followed his cousin up the front steps of the Stoke

Bruerne home, trepidation coursing through his veins. Eloise was somewhere on the other side of that door, and he must act as though he had no interest in her as anything other than his cousin's potential bride. How could he possibly do that? He'd frozen in the middle of a crowded ballroom, in the center of the dance floor no less when he'd been struck by nothing less than her ethereal beauty.

He went to rake his hand through his hair in frustration but instead nearly toppled off his beaver hat. He caught it just in time and fixed it back into place, but Liam had noticed and eyed him suspiciously.

"Lady Stoke Bruerne is attempting to coax her other daughter, the widow Wexford, back into society and thought having her join us would be a good first step toward that endeavor." Here Liam poked Tuck directly in the chest. "Lady Stoke Bruerne also thought you'd make an excellent promenading partner for the widow. I believe she said you were perfectly pleasant." Liam raised both eyebrows, a grin flirting with his lips.

"I'm glad you're enjoying this. I should be at The Royal Astronomical Society trying to find a benefactor."

Liam's eyebrows dropped. "Oh, come now. You mustn't be like that." His cousin paused, and his expression was almost kind as he puzzled something out. "I think being seen as perfectly pleasant is rather a compliment."

Tuck turned about and had taken the first step back toward the pavement when his cousin grabbed his shoulder.

"I take it back," Liam said quickly. "I take it back." Tuck turned only his head to eye Liam as the man lifted a hand in supplication. "I promise to take you to my club tonight for its weekly poker game. There will be a lot of wealthy men there with a lot of money they would never miss."

"Poker?"

Liam waved a hand dismissively. "It's an American game.

Much fun. You'll enjoy it." He moved that hand now to press against his chest in earnest. "I just ask this one thing of you."

"You already asked me to dance with Lady Eloise," Tuck pointed out.

Liam dropped the hand, blinking. "I suppose I did. But that was to get your opinion of the girl. That was very important to me, and I can't tell you how much I appreciate the sacrifice."

"She isn't a girl." Tuck didn't know why he said that or why he said it quite so loudly and with such conviction. He shut his mouth and averted his gaze but not before he caught a curious look on his cousin's face.

"I see," Liam muttered. "Then you'll accompany me?"

Tuck stepped back up onto the stoop and waved a hand. "Get on with it then."

Liam's smile was not unlike that of a tomcat who caught his mouse. Tuck clenched his fingers into a fist to keep from knocking off his hat again trying to run his fingers through his hair.

The butler opened the door of the Stoke Bruerne home before Liam's knuckles had even touched the door. The servant bid them enter and informed them the ladies Stoke Bruerne were waiting in the drawing room.

Tuck took one last deep breath of fresh air and plunged in after his cousin. Perhaps Lady Eloise wouldn't be quite so enchanting in the light of day. He'd only ever seen her under circumstances that were by design overwhelmingly romantic —beneath a blanket of stars or the glow of a thousand chandeliers. Perhaps it wasn't quite a thousand, but it had certainly felt like it.

Maybe when he saw her in a perfectly ordinary drawing room in daylight she herself would appear perfectly ordinary as well.

Yes, that was just it. He needn't worry in the least. Everything was going to be—

His first glimpse of her as he walked through the drawing room door behind his cousin stole his breath. He had always thought the phrase a silly one, but just then he knew it to be true. His breath lodged in his throat, nearly choking him as she rose to greet him.

She stared right at him. Not at Liam as she should have done. But him. Tuck. A simple mister.

Her eyes found him so swiftly, he thought she could find him anywhere, the connection between them too strong to ever be severed. Oh God, this was a very bad idea.

"Mr. Ryan, I can't thank you enough for joining my daughters today. It is such a fine day, is it not?"

It was a moment before Tuck realized greetings had been exchanged, and Lady Stoke Bruerne was addressing him. He was still trying to determine how that green frock Eloise wore could make her eyes shine like jewels, make her hair glow like sunshine. It must have been an illusion, a trick of the light, or—

"Yes." The word came out garbled, and he cleared his throat to try again. "Yes, it is a particularly fine day."

When he'd first learned he was to accompany Liam today, he had wished for rain, a monsoon really, but the day had dawned bright and clear with the gentlest breeze to keep a promenader from growing overtaxed. It *was* particularly perfect, blast it.

Lady Stoke Bruerne smiled and clapped her hands together. "Well, please don't let me keep you from your exercise."

There was the general commotion of gathering wraps and parasols then as their party moved back into the foyer from the drawing room. But before they could reach the front door, a small hand descended on Tuck's arm. He nearly jumped out of his skin as he was so consumed by the anxiety of facing an entire afternoon with Eloise, and he wasn't prepared for someone to suddenly touch him.

He looked down to find a stooped old woman holding his arm. While her back was hunched and her hair was a brilliant white, her eyes were bright and worse, they were focused on him. She tugged at his arm, drawing him down so she could whisper in his ear.

"My granddaughter seeks adventure. Only you can stop her from being trapped in a drawing room." The woman's voice was brittle with age, but her words were sure and precise. She said nothing more. She didn't even look at him. She simply released his arm and turned about, ambling down the corridor into the bowels of the house at a sedate pace.

Tuck watched her go, the trepidation that had been boiling inside of him suddenly stilling as curiosity overtook it. Her granddaughter sought adventure? Did the old woman—Tuck must assume the woman was the Stoke Bruerne grandmother—refer to Eloise? And what sort of adventure? Why must Tuck be the one to save her? Save her from what?

He was prevented from getting lost in the cryptic information from Eloise's grandmother as the group departed without him, leaving him to trail after them down the front stoop to the pavement below. Eloise had taken Liam's arm as she should have done, and Tuck took his place beside Lady Wexford who as of yet had not spoken a single word. She wore mourning clothes, although not as severe as some he'd seen. Her gown was a muted lavender, and her bonnet was trimmed with dark velvet and shrouded her face.

Was Eloise speaking a little too quickly? Were her gestures a little too animated? Perhaps he was simply comparing her to the mute Lady Wexford, and such a comparison was by its nature extreme.

He swallowed. "It is a rather fine day, isn't it, Lady Wexford?"

The poor woman stumbled the smallest bit, and her head snapped up as if no one had ever asked her a question. He reached out instinctively to break her fall, but she jerked out of his reach, almost like an involuntary reaction.

He nearly stopped walking, concern for this poor woman rising inside of him. Her eyes were huge in her face as she blinked at him, and he saw real pain in her expression. Liam had said Lady Stoke Bruerne was attempting to get the woman to reenter society, but standing there, Tuck believed she was not ready to give up her grieving.

He held up both hands and gestured for her to continue walking. He didn't say anything more.

The walk to the park was uneventful. Traffic was light, the walking paths not overcrowded, and the breeze gentle against his face. It was all so damn perfect. Eloise and Liam continued their chatter, each exchanging anecdotes followed by polite laughter until Tuck thought he might be sick in the bushes.

They only stopped occasionally in their promenade when they crossed paths with an acquaintance. Pleasantries were exchanged, and their party continued, Liam and Eloise happily bubbling along while Tuck tried very hard to keep Lady Wexford from shrinking entirely into herself.

Liam and Eloise were several steps ahead of them now, and he swallowed, drawing a careful breath. "I once lost someone very dear to me," he said. "It was quite a long time ago now, and I wish I could tell you the pain goes away, but it doesn't." He gathered his courage and glanced at Lady Wexford to find her staring at him. Her eyes were still wide, but it was as though she were absorbing him rather than afraid of him. He went on. "I wish I could say one day you'll wake up and not have that one moment where you believe everything is all right until you remember that it's not." He paused, watching a flock of birds suddenly take flight from a far-off tree, swooping into the sky in perfect formation. "But that doesn't happen. Time only wears away the edges of grief. It doesn't wear it away completely." He glanced at Lady Wexford again, and he found her expression had softened. "Your grief may not disappear, but you will learn to carry it more easily." He smiled, hoping to ease his words, but then Lady Wexford did the oddest thing. She smiled.

"I believe my mother is right about you, Mr. Ryan."

Tuck worked to keep his expression from showing the very real fear that gripped him. "How is that?"

Lady Wexford's smile brightened. "You are perfectly pleasant."

His smile was forced and only half what he meant it to be, but he was saved from having to respond when he realized Liam and Eloise had stopped. At some point in his awkward exchange with the widow Wexford, they'd arrived at the Serpentine, and Liam stood on the lakeshore, gazing out over the water.

"Do you know I think it's a perfect day for a water excursion?" He turned back to their group, his smile not unlike the time he suggested Tuck join him in sneaking out of the nursery in the middle of the night to watch a meteor shower. "What say you we hire a pair of rowing boats for an hour?"

Tuck risked a glance at Lady Wexford, sure she would faint dead away at this suggestion, but again, she surprised him by saying, "That would be wonderful, Your Grace. I should think the conditions are absolutely pristine for such an endeavor."

Liam's smile broadened. "Splendid. I shall see to it at once." His cousin spun about and down to the dock where the boat hire was, leaving Tuck with the two ladies.

As soon as Liam departed, Eloise's animated expression

vanished, and she turned wary eyes on him. He stared right back at her. It wasn't as though this was his doing. He had meant it when he agreed to stay away from her. She'd been right after all. They had no business pursuing this connection that had sprung up between them. It wasn't practical.

So why then would Eloise's grandmother tell him about her granddaughter's desire for adventure?

"Shall we?" he said, gesturing to the path that led down to the docks. By the time they reached the platform, two rowing boats had been drawn up and tied securely for the parties to enter them safely.

Liam finished his dealings with the boatman and returned in time to help Eloise into the boat, saving Tuck from having to touch her. Except Liam didn't help Eloise. Instead, he reached for Lady Wexford's arm.

"Lady Wexford, would you do me the honor of joining me? I think your sister deserves a break from all my chattering, don't you?"

Lady Wexford smiled again and took the duke's arm. "I would never suggest you're one to chatter, Your Grace, but I shall be honored to join you for a turn about the lake."

She was nestled into the boat with Liam removing the ties before Tuck could utter a single word in protest.

"Happy rowing," Liam called back to them as he jumped lightly into the boat, pushing it from the dock. He smiled at Tuck and waved a jovial hand in departure, but there was nothing jovial about it. Tuck recognized that look in Liam's eye. It was the same one that had gotten Tuck to engage in all manner of things, usually ones which required a stern lecture from his father afterward.

"What is he doing?" Eloise hissed beside him.

"He's being Liam," Tuck answered, taking her arm. "Get in the boat before we attract attention."

She did as he bid, lifting her skirts to step swiftly over the edge of the boat before lowering herself to the bench. He tried not to think about how long it had been since he'd touched her—four whole days—or how she smelled of soap and fresh linen as if she were comprised of all things good and wholesome. He untied the boat and hopped in, picking up the oars to push them away from the dock and into the lake proper.

He focused on rowing, following in the general direction of Liam and Lady Wexford's boat while keeping enough distance to not appear suspicious.

"This is very bad," Eloise said when they were far enough from shore not to be overheard by other patrons of the park.

"I promise to keep my hands on the oars," Tuck muttered, keeping his voice low.

"It isn't that," Eloise whispered back. "If people see us like this, there will be talk. We must appear to be having a terrible time."

His focus snapped at that, his gaze flying to her face. "I don't think it's possible to have a terrible time with you, Eloise."

She'd been about to say something else, but she stopped at that, her lips forming the words she never spoke. It was several seconds before she looked away, her eyes scanning the lakeshore. He forced his attention back to the rowing until she spoke again.

"Tell me something about your research. Why the aurora borealis? Why telegraph communication?"

He didn't move his gaze from the oars and where he was steering them, not trusting himself to look at her. "Why do you wish to know?"

"I'm hoping the topic is terribly dry and boring. Dry and boring could never be construed as romantic."

"I have never been accused of being romantic," Tuck muttered.

Eloise turned her head at this, and he caught the smile she tried to hide. "I find that hard to believe."

"I scared away a vicar the other day," he said and felt the tension ease from his shoulders as they fell into a less perilous conversation.

"A vicar?"

"I was attempting to explain the reasons for my expedition."

"To study the aurora? I should hardly think that a frightening prospect." She tilted her head, catching a ray of sun over the brim of her bonnet so it lit her face like a spotlight. She was so damn pretty it hurt.

"It was to the vicar."

She adjusted on the seat, and he noticed she clutched her hands in her lap as if she were trying to keep herself from touching him. "Tell me about your reasons for your expedition, Mr. Ryan. I am certain I shall find them terrifyingly boring, and all romantic notions we might have had will vanish entirely." Her tone held a note of teasing, but there was some truth in her words. If he spoke only of his professional pursuits, there could be no room for romantic entanglements.

Except when he looked at her, the sunshine lighting her face, the smallest of breezes lifting the mossy green ribbon of her bonnet, he found himself saying the thing he had sworn never to say.

"I wish to study the effect of the aurora borealis because in the Carrington Event of 1859, telegraph communications were interrupted by the solar storm, and my brother Harrison was killed because he did not receive a telegram containing critical information that might have saved his life."

CHAPTER 5

$\mathcal{W}$ ell, there was nothing terrifyingly boring about that.

"Oh God, Tuck, I'm so sorry." The words escaped her lips before she knew she would call him by his given name, but as the water gently rocked their rowboat and a spring breeze caressed her cheek, she didn't think she could very well call him anything else.

His gaze skittered away from her, and she worried if she'd upset him. Without thinking, she reached out and placed her hand over his against the oar.

"I'm sorry, Tuck," she said again with more emphasis. "You mustn't speak of it if you don't wish to."

His attention came back to her, and she was surprised to find curiosity in his features rather than annoyance.

"It's odd, but I think I feel better having told you that." His hand worked the oar beneath hers as if he needed to do something physical while he sorted through his emotions. "I've never told anyone about Harrison. Anyone who didn't already know." He paused, his eyes changing as he considered her. "I'm glad you know now."

"I'm glad I know too," she said and let go of his hand to sit up on her bench. "Do you wish to speak of it? Perhaps that will feel good as well."

He looked away again, and she wondered if that was a habit, a way for him to collect his thoughts before speaking. When he turned back to her, a small smile played at his lips.

"Harrison was twelve years older than me and the second born son to my parents. There is a sister next, and my mother lost a baby after my sister. So I'm a good deal younger than my siblings, but Harrison never seemed to mind. He never treated me like an annoyance. If anything, he went out of his way to ensure I had a fun and at times adventurous childhood." He swallowed then, so abruptly it looked almost painful, and she couldn't stop herself from reaching out again and taking his hand.

This time she plucked it from the oar and cradled it between both of her own. The little rowboat bobbed in the water, the breeze pushing it along the lake. She was no longer paying attention to where the wind carried them. She could only study Tuck's face, watch the past play out across his features.

"He went into service as was expected of him." He looked up then and met her eyes as if remembering suddenly she was there. "Our father is a very minor baron and a judge, and my mother is the daughter of a viscount. My brother was expected to either take up the cloth or enlist, and as he was not ever one for Bible study, he chose the Queen's Navy instead." Her hand involuntarily clenched as she connected the pieces in her mind and braced herself for what was to come. "My brother was to sail on the *Imogene* out of Portsmouth. It was loaded with supplies for the Cape Colony. Another Navy ship, the *Chilton*, had passed through the Mediterranean just days before on its way to India through the Suez Canal. They encountered a storm unlike any they had seen before. They'd made it into port before the storm could take their ship, and they sent a telegram back to Portsmouth to delay the departure of the *Imogene*." His eyes were on hers again, and she could almost feel the aching sadness that rippled through him. "The telegram didn't reach Portsmouth because of the solar storm. My brother's ship left port, my brother on it. It sank two days later before it even reached the African coast. All souls perished."

She didn't know how she didn't break his hand with the way her grip tightened, as if she could make it all better simply by holding on to him.

"I'm so sorry," she said, never before feeling how useless such words could be.

She couldn't bring back his brother or any of the other souls lost that day when the *Imogene* sank. But worse, she couldn't take away his pain in the here and now, and that hurt more than anything at the same time she was in awe of it. For a man of science like Tuck to feel something so deeply, so completely, and to rearrange his life around those feelings, was something truly extraordinary.

He let go of the other oar then and placed his hand on top of hers, and now she couldn't be sure who held whom. "I can't let it happen again, Eloise." His eyes flashed to hers, and she saw the determination in there, a determination that spoke to her, setting fire to parts of herself she had thought wasted. The yearning for a purpose, the desire for a mission, the need for more. But it was right there in his eyes, all of it. And she could never have it.

Still. She leaned in, unable to look away, unable to give up what she saw there. Maybe later she would be strong enough, but right now all of him simmered at the surface, and she wanted to dive in.

"I can't let it happen again," he repeated, more softly this time. "I promised myself, and I promised my mother and father that I would stop it from happening to someone else's brother, someone else's son. And that's why I must find the funds for my expedition."

She shook her head. "Then why don't you tell people about Harrison? You said you never spoke of him."

His eyes grew dark then, impossibly so, and she wondered at their changeability. "Because I don't want this to be about him. It feels like I'm capitalizing on his loss to suit my own needs. I won't sell him for a pound."

While the sadness in his voice had been palpable when he'd relayed the story of his brother's death, the vehemence in his tone now was enough to cut iron.

"You're not selling him," she said. "You're making sure his death wasn't meaningless."

Something sharp passed over his face then, and it was almost as though she'd slapped him, light coming into his eyes when there'd only been darkness. But he didn't speak, and neither did she. Silence fell over them like a fog, and it was as though he became her entire world. Everything came to a point where they held each other, and all she had to do was lean forward and press her lips to his, and he would be hers forever. She knew that somehow even as she knew she could never do it.

But right then she could. She remembered what it had been like to kiss him. It was like the flowery prose of fairy tales or the exotic ramblings of a novel. Kissing Tucker Ryan was simply what she was meant to do. It felt like coming home when she hadn't known she'd been away.

So she leaned forward or maybe he leaned toward her. She closed her eyes, and then—

She was unceremoniously knocked from the rowboat.

One moment she was nearing heaven and the next she was all but drowning.

She wasn't sure what hurt more. When the giant hairy

creature struck her or when she hit the water after tumbling from the rowboat. Either way the shock of it dulled her senses until she was under the dark, murky water of the Serpentine, her lungs burning for air even as water rushed up her nose, and her skirts clamped down on her legs as though they wished to drown her.

She had no sense of direction, but it needn't matter anyway as her dress had successfully trapped her legs, preventing her from propelling herself to the surface. It didn't stop her from trying though, forcing her eyes open to see if she could find the light of the surface and turn her body toward it.

But just as she got her eyes open, the water erupted in an explosion. The surge lifted her even as strong arms wrapped around her like a steel cage. When she broke through the surface, her lungs sucked in air automatically, ravenous for oxygen as the brilliant sun blinded her. Someone was yelling, the sound echoing through the water still filling her ears. It was several seconds before she could interpret what was being said.

"Put your feet down."

Again the motion was automatic, and her legs went rigid, standing her straight up until—

Her feet sank in a cushion of mud, stopping abruptly and allowing her to stand. Through the curtain of water that poured down her face, she became aware of several things. She was standing in the Serpentine, in approximately—she looked down—three feet of water, the whole of which she thought would drown her. Their little rowboat rocked violently before her as if upset by a sudden motion, and beyond it, the shore was crowded with gawkers.

"Oh," she said, the word little more than a sound of despair as she took in the crowd.

"Oh God."

She swung about to find Tuck in the water beside her. He was only soaked to the waist and the sleeves of his jacket as he'd reached into the water to pull her up. He shucked that jacket now as if it were on fire and swung it about her so quickly, she nearly toppled over into the water again. Without waiting for her to respond, he yanked the opening of the jacket together, drawing her smack into his chest.

"Oof," she mumbled, peering up at him from her precarious position in his grip. "What are you doing?" she hissed.

She did a lot of hissing with him. Was this how their relationship was to be? Would they always find themselves in scandalous situations that required discreet whispering?

"You're wet."

"Of course, I'm—" She stopped talking, realization setting in. She glanced down even though all she could see were Tuck's fisted hands as he held his jacket in place in front of her bosom. A bosom that likely had been clearly outlined for all of the onlookers to gaze upon. "Thank you," she finished and carefully pried Tuck's hands loose to assume control of the jacket that shielded her more private bits from the gawkers.

But he didn't let go. She looked up, questioning, only to find something in his eyes she'd never seen there before.

Desire.

Pure, molten desire.

It was so unexpected the breath caught in her throat, and she was very much afraid of drowning again. While she had always felt a magical rightness with Tuck, she'd never felt his passion the way she did now, and it truly stole her breath. Her body responded to the look in his eyes without her volition, muscles clenching, heart racing. Longing was one thing. Desire was something else entirely.

And it broke her heart all over again.

This man wasn't hers to have. No matter how he desired her and how she wanted him. It wasn't to be.

"Tuck." His name was enough to break the spell, and he released her, taking her elbow beneath the jacket to help her to shore.

"I'm so sorry," a voice called from the lakeside. "He's never done that before. I don't know what came over him."

She blinked against the sun, trying to make out the voice who called to her in apology.

"That's quite all right," she said as the speaker came into view.

It was a woman slightly older than she, perhaps somewhere in her thirties. A gaggle of children stood behind her and one of them, a boy who towered above the rest with long limbs and floppy dark hair, held a dog who dripped water much as Eloise imagined she did. The boy had wrapped both arms around the animal as if giving him a tight hug to keep the animal from bounding forward. Again, it would seem.

"He doesn't usually chase waterfowl," the woman said now. "I mean..." She cast a worried eye at the dog. "He's afraid of sheep."

They'd reached the shore then, and a gentleman there reached down to pull her up the bank.

"He *is* afraid of sheep," the gentleman said now. "To that I can attest. Piglets too." He held up a finger when she was safely on both of her feet on the firmness of land. "Not pigs, mind you. Just the piglets."

She realized suddenly this man was with this woman, and this gaggle of children must be theirs. Her heart squeezed suddenly, and tears threatened as the yearning she'd tried to tamp down rose up inside of her.

This was what she'd wanted. This big happy brood of a

family, spending their days together and creating memories like this one.

The time the family dog nearly drowned a lady in the Serpentine.

She smiled even though her heart trembled. "It's really quite all right. I assure you no harm's been done." No harm that was visible anyway.

The woman stepped forward now, touching her husband's elbow with a familiarity that spoke to how often she'd done it. A thousand times? More?

"I'm Eliza Kane, the Duchess of Ashbourne. You must allow me to procure a new gown for you." The woman's face was twisted with concern, sending a pair of small gold spectacles climbing up her nose.

Eloise only waved the suggestion away. "I assure you no such thing is necessary. I don't usually partake of a swim so early in the season, but I suppose one must remain flexible."

Eloise couldn't accept this woman's kindness because the guilt would kill her. The truth of it was this woman's dog had saved Eloise from scandal. She'd almost kissed Tuck in that little rowboat in front of all these people. She'd have been ruined for sure. Tuck never would have secured a benefactor then. A man who damaged the reputation of a debutante? He'd be seen as no more than a scoundrel.

The duchess did not look convinced, but before Eloise could reassure her, a commotion at the back of the crowd had them turning.

Ardley pushed through the gathering, Annie trailing behind him.

"Eloise," she said as soon as she reached them. "Are you hurt?"

Eloise smiled and shook her head, sending water droplets about her like a fountain. "Not in the least. It seems I'm merely the victim of normal canine instincts."

"Ashbourne," Ardley said then. "What the devil are you doing here? I thought it took an act of Parliament to get you out of that home of yours on the ocean."

Ashbourne gave a bark of laughter. "Hardly an act of Parliament, Ardley. Just visiting family, I'm afraid. Another niece is being christened. Wouldn't miss it for anything."

"Another one? How many does that make?"

"Eleven," the duchess answered, her tone flat.

Eloise felt a tug of commiseration. Eleven nieces were a lot. She could only wonder at the number of nephews that might be involved and thought it best not to ask.

"Are you sure there's nothing I can do?" the duchess asked then. "I promise you he's normally a well-behaved dog."

"He's twelve years old. This is the most exciting thing he's done in ages," Ashbourne added.

Again Eloise waved them off. "Think nothing of it. Nothing has happened that can't be remedied."

That wasn't exactly the truth, and much later when she gave Tuck his jacket back, they were both very careful not to touch one another.

* * *

HE WAS AT LEAST DRY when the summons arrived.

He'd bathed and dressed faster than he'd thought possible, not wishing to be alone with his thoughts for longer than was necessary and was descending the stairs of Ardley House when a footman stopped him. A lad had come to the kitchen door with a note for the Honorable Mr. Tucker Ryan.

Tuck eyed the folded note on the footman's silver salver as if it were a slumbering cobra. He had no wish to prod it, but the footman said the lad was waiting for a response.

Without delay, he snatched up the paper and read the two words scribbled across it.

Courtyard. Midnight.

There was no greeting or signature, but he didn't need one. He knew who had sent such a cryptic message and knew all too well what it meant.

It was absolutely the worst idea he'd ever heard of, so he raised his eyes to the footman and said, "Yes, of course."

The footman nodded and bounded back down the stairs to give the reply to the waiting messenger boy. Putting the note in his pocket with one hand, Tuck ran his other hand through his hair and went down the remainder of the stairs to find something to distract him. Perhaps there was a circus of monkeys in the drawing room doing acrobats. That would probably keep him occupied for a few minutes.

He found nothing in the drawing room and no one there either. Retracing his steps back into the hall, he found the butler lurking.

"His Grace wished me to inform you he went out for the evening. He had urgent business, which required his attention," Mansfield explained.

Urgent business? Tuck thought it likely involved a woman.

He forced a smile. "Thank you, Mansfield. Would you please have a tray brought up to the library? I think I shall read for a bit."

He didn't read. He knew he wouldn't. He paced instead. Paced, ruminated, stewed, and paced some more. The tray Mansfield sent up went untouched except for the tea, which he drank by the pot, forcing the poor maid to refill the thing by the hour, but his pacing fueled quite a thirst.

What was he going to do about Eloise?

The plan to ignore her clearly wasn't going to work, not with Liam courting her. They were likely to be thrown together for the whole of the season, and they must come up with a better plan than avoidance.

But what would the plan be when Liam and Eloise finally wed?

This thought stopped him completely.

What *would* he do?

He had his research. Perhaps that would be enough to keep him from London, keep him from having to witness Eloise married to someone else. Not just someone. Tuck's cousin. *Liam.*

He shoved a hand through his hair. God, he'd made a mess of this. But to be fair, he hadn't known he was doing anything. Eloise had just been a lady he'd encountered under the stars one night. How was he to know who she really was?

His research wouldn't keep him from London forever. Besides he couldn't fathom a life spent away from Liam.

Hell's teeth, he couldn't see a way out of this. His only hope was that his feelings for her would fade, that one day he wouldn't feel that instant clench of his gut when he saw her, as though his body recognized her without his conscious mind doing so, as if it...*knew.*

Cursing, he turned and looked at the clock on the mantel. Half eight. Midnight was an eternity away.

He collapsed on the nearest sofa, the will to even pace having drained out of him. He lay there and contemplated a life without Liam, a life without Eloise, and wondered how on earth he'd gotten into this predicament. He had already been in London for almost a month, and he was without benefactor and quite possibly soon he'd lose his cousin and the woman who had snared his passion all in one go. Could it get any worse?

It could, in fact. When the clock struck eleven, he realized with a start he must have fallen asleep at some point. He scrubbed the sleep from his face and rose, straightening himself as best he could before heading out of the library.

Ardley House was one of the newer homes in Mayfair with a shared courtyard with the other houses along the block. The courtyard was accessed through a set of doors off the conservatory. He'd discovered it when he'd first arrived and was seeking some outside space to use for some of the smaller experiments he'd brought with him, including the stargazing glasses he'd been testing the night he'd first encountered Eloise.

He slipped through the conservatory now and out into the night. They were deep into spring and unlike that night in early March, the air was warm against his cheek, having lost its winter bite over the past few weeks. He wound his way through the hedges at the edge of the terrace and onto the path that would lead to the heart of the courtyard.

The gardens there were of simple design, mostly yew hedges, the occasional flowering tree, firs and some sturdier trees to provide shade, and benches were placed along designated paths at specific intervals. The space was one very much suited to taking in the air rather than any serious gardening endeavors, and he found he enjoyed it. Such a clean, common space in which to enjoy both the outdoors and one's neighbors. It was no wonder Ardley had chosen to sell the previous London townhome and purchase the lease here when he'd become duke.

The thought made his heart hurt, thinking of his cousin like that, and he pushed it away. Tuck was Odysseus himself, sailing between the dangers that lurked before him, and he liked none of his options.

Eloise was already in the spot where he'd first seen her, and the sight of her standing in much the same way as she'd been when he'd happened upon her the first time sent his stomach twisting with anticipation and nostalgia. Nostalgia. God, what was wrong with him?

"Eloise." He spoke her name softly, reluctantly, not wishing to break the moment as she gazed so wondrously at the stars.

Her head turned swiftly though, her eyes falling on him, but her expression never changed. She kept that same wondrous gaze about her, and he wondered if that was how she approached the world, with a sense of curiosity and exploration.

"Tuck." Her voice held a smile he somehow knew she was holding back.

"I'm sorry about today—" he started, but she held up a hand, cutting him off.

"There's no need to apologize. You didn't knock me into the lake." The smile came now, slow but sure.

He wasn't apologizing for the dousing she had received. Not entirely. The apology was more for how he had felt at seeing her standing there beside him, her every curve outlined. She'd gone from the woman who had infatuated him to a woman he very much desired in the space of seconds. When she was just Eloise, the mysterious woman under the stars, she had held a mystical element that had kept her almost untouchable. Even though he had kissed her, she still seemed otherworldly.

But when he'd seen her, all of her, she'd become real to him, solid, attainable.

"I should have stopped the dog."

She raised an eyebrow. "And both of us would have taken a swim."

She was probably right, so he went on. "If it's not an apology you're seeking, why did you ask me to meet you here?"

Her expression dimmed then, and he wished he could

snatch back his words. She turned to fully face him, and he noticed her hands were folded in front of her in an efficient manner that didn't seem to fit with the rest he knew of her.

"I don't think our plan is going to work."

He held back his own smile. "I came to the very same conclusion. What do you suggest we do?"

She took a step toward him and then another. He should have stepped aside, moved past her, but he couldn't. His feet remained fixed to the path as he watched her approach.

"If we can't avoid each other, we must come to an understanding."

"An understanding?"

She was close enough now that he could see the gold tones in her hair. She wore no bonnet, and he drank in the sight of her, all of her. The tumble of her hair as it had loosened from some of its pins, how her eyes flashed in the moonlight, how her shoulders relaxed the closer she came, an easiness settling over her.

"You have something I need, and I have something you need."

"Something you need?"

She licked her lips and looked down at her toes for a second before meeting his gaze and saying quickly, "I must secure Ardley's hand this season."

It was like a bullet directly to his heart, but she likely knew that. She'd been swift in her delivery, and it had caused him the least damage. The wound her words left was only fatal.

"And what do you have?" He didn't want to talk about her marrying Liam.

Now her smile came easily. "I will help you find a benefactor."

"Is that so? I'm afraid you're too late. The Duke of

Grimsby has offered his aid," he said as the duke had indeed offered to help Tuck in his endeavor.

Her smile didn't falter. In fact, she gave a small laugh. "Grimsby doesn't have what I have."

"And what is that?"

She held out her arms. "My charm."

The way she said it, with warmth and humility, had him laughing. "Your charm?"

She dropped her arms. "And connections. The Stoke Bruerne name is a respected one. I can help you with introductions." She poked him in the chest with a single finger. "And you can tell Ardley what a reliable helpmate I am."

Her finger didn't leave his chest. He stared it, and she stared at it, and they both said nothing, not for several seconds.

"Helpmate?" he finally managed, but still her finger didn't move. Or rather it didn't leave his chest.

Her hand shifted, coming to lie flat against him, the tips of her fingers curling ever so slightly into the front of his jacket as if she were testing something, searching for something.

"Hmm." She made a distracted noise, and her gaze was on her hand, which moved freely now, sliding up until it reached the tangle of his cravat, higher until her fingertips touched the heat of his skin just above his shirt collar. Her touch was tentative, merely a brush, and then her hand stilled.

Just like it had in the boat earlier that day when he had felt as though the entire universe came to a point at the exact spot where they touched.

Her eyes lifted to meet his. "We make this a kind of partnership, Mr. Ryan."

"Partnership." Were her eyes brown or hazel? In the

moonlight he could have sworn there were streaks of forest green in them.

"I help you." She moved her hand, the barest of touches skimming his jaw, and electricity coursed through him until he thought it would render him paralyzed. "You help me."

He couldn't take any more. He seized her, lifting her off her feet, backing her up until he pressed her against a tree. He kissed her then, his mouth crushing hers as her arms came around his neck, her fingers clawing at his hair.

"I. Help. You." He pronounced each word between biting kisses along her jaw, her neck, her earlobe.

"I. Help. You." She responded in kind, pushing her head back against the tree trunk as far as she could, lifting her chin, exposing the long line of her neck to him.

He took, first pressing his mouth to the place that throbbed with her pulse and then running his tongue up the column of her neck until she whimpered, one leg coming up to wrap around him, pulling him even closer to her.

He ached. Every part of him ached and yearned for her, but he'd already taken too much.

"I want you." She whispered the words. They skated over his ear and passed directly to his heart.

Suddenly nothing else mattered. Not society. Not a benefactor. Not even Liam.

Eloise was alive in his arms, and it was like he was seeing the world for the very first time after a long period of darkness. She had done that. She had opened him like that.

He *felt*. After spending so long in his dead brother's shadow, Tuck felt something other than the urgency to avenge Harrison's death. He felt her, Eloise, and it was almost more than he could bear.

He kissed her. He drank her in. It was as though she were the elixir of life and he the dying man. He couldn't explain it or understand it, and he didn't want to. He just wanted to keep kissing her, keep holding her, keep exploring her.

His hands ran down her torso, over her hips, and around to her buttocks, pulling her against him even though it was impossible for them to get any closer, but he must try. He *must*.

His hand roamed farther, lower, deeper. He cradled her thigh in his palm, kneaded it until she moaned against his mouth. The sound drove his desire into a fury, and he needed more. He needed all of her.

His fingers worked at her skirts, pulling them up inch by painful inch. When his fingers closed around the angles of her knee, he nearly lost what little sense he had left. She wore silk stockings, and his fingers slid along her knee, tracing the outline higher and higher until he stumbled into the line of lace at the top.

He paused, lingered, savored. Another inch and he would find bare skin. He knew that, and yet he couldn't make his hand move. Not yet. He let the anticipation build, let the blood thrum through his veins, let his body shake with need for her.

Only then did he move his hand, sliding it up, tracing the pattern of lace until—

She sucked in a breath, the sound sharp in the quiet of the night, when his fingers found her bare thigh.

"Tuck." His name was little more than a whimper, and it was almost his undoing.

That he could do this to her, that he could make her want, that he could pleasure her.

Suddenly he needed to see her. He needed to see what he did to her.

Pulling ever so slowly away, he studied her, her head thrown back against the tree, her face flush, heat rising up her neck as she took harsh, ragged breaths. His gaze lingered there only a moment before dropping to his hand, to the place where flesh met flesh, and he finally touched her as he longed to touch her.

He saw it, his hand against her thigh, and desire roared up in him at the same time something else did. A realization, a thought, an understanding.

Forbidden.

He wrenched his hand away, took a stumbling step backward, and shoved the shaking hand through his hair.

And before she could open her eyes, before she could utter a single word in protest, he said, "Good night, Eloise," and stumbled off into the dark.

CHAPTER 6

"If you push that bit of sausage around your plate one more time, I shall summon a vicar to perform an exorcism on your beleaguered soul. Perhaps Templeton is available."

Tuck looked up from his breakfast plate to find Liam appearing to be deep in the morning papers. Obviously his cousin wasn't for he hadn't failed to notice Tuck's unsettled state. They were in the breakfast room of Ardley House, having both risen at an unusually early hour as the previous night's festivities included only a musicale, which had bless-edly ended at a reasonable hour.

Tuck set his fork aside. "I'm sorry, cousin. My mind's rather full this morning."

Full of Eloise. Full of her taste. Full of her smell. Full of her.

It had been nearly a week since that night in the court-yard, yet it felt as though it had been only hours ago that he had touched her, that he had nearly taken her. Betrayal cut through him, and he pushed his plate away.

Liam folded the paper on the table beside his own empty plate. "Is this because of Grimsby's offer?"

It was a moment before Tuck remembered of what his cousin spoke. Grimsby's offer to help Tuck find a benefactor.

"I've been through your copy of Debrett's, and I'm afraid I'm none the wiser," Tuck said.

Liam's brow wrinkled. "I can't imagine. I've never looked at the thing," he said, folding his paper and setting it aside to lean forward. "I have a hunch Debrett's is not what's occupying such space in your thoughts this morning." He paused, but Tuck didn't speak, knowing his cousin well enough to understand the man wasn't finished. And he wasn't. "I think the murkiness of your mind has more to do with Lady Eloise and what happened at the Serpentine last week."

Tuck sat up, tossing aside his napkin. "I have apologized for that. I didn't expect a dog to send your perspective bride into the lake."

There was much more for which Tuck should apologize, but instead of speaking of it, he let it burn a hole through his gut.

Liam waved his words away just as he'd done every time Tuck had tried to apologize in the past several days since that affair on the Serpentine.

"You know I don't blame you for that. Lady Eloise was unharmed, and I got to act the knight gallant by escorting her home." Liam's smile was self-satisfied. "It couldn't have gone any better, I should think." He seemed to consider his words before continuing. "I think there's something else about the lady that is plaguing you this morning, cousin. Do you wish to speak of it?"

Tuck saw the opportunity to change the subject and took it. "I've been in London for more than a month now, and I have zero prospects for a benefactor."

Liam blinked. "Is that all?"

Tuck pushed back his chair, suddenly needing to stand. "Is that all?" he repeated. "That is the very reason I came to London in the first place." He strode over to the windows at the end of the table and peered out on the street. It was still relatively quiet at this hour, a single hackney traveling toward the crossroad. "I need to secure a benefactor before the summer, or I'll never have time to prepare for the expedition." He turned around to look at his cousin. "I'll miss another season of the aurora borealis if I don't find a funder soon."

Liam leaned back in his chair, propping one foot on the opposite knee as he steepled his fingers together, elbows resting on the arms of his chair. "This is my fault. I've been distracting you with my search for a bride."

Tuck felt the instant sting of guilt. "It's not that," he said. "You know I'm happy to help you in any way I can." He stopped there, feeling the guilt grow inside of him and morph into something else entirely.

That sick feeling of betrayal he hadn't been able to shake since that first ball of the season, the one where he'd realized his feelings for his cousin's prospective bride were not innocent. That alone had been enough, but now he'd acted on those feelings.

"I know that, but I shouldn't allow your altruism to get in the way of your endeavor."

Tuck was truly going to be sick at the word *altruism*.

Was it altruism that had him kissing Eloise? That had him holding her hands in a very public setting where had they been caught the scandal would have not only ruined Eloise but likely Liam by connection? By taking her the way he had against a tree of all things? Was that what altruism was?

He swallowed and paced back to the windows. If they had been caught...

It would have been over then. He would have been forced to wed Eloise to save her reputation, and his cousin would never forgive him. How could Tuck have been so stupid? He could never let such a slip happen again.

He ran a frustrated hand through his hair. "I guess I just thought it would be easier to secure a benefactor." He turned back to Liam who still lounged in his chair. "Isn't the prospect of understanding how solar storms affect modern communication an important field to explore?"

Liam blinked. "I'm sorry. I fear I may have fallen asleep there."

Tuck frowned, and Liam laughed, dropping his feet to the floor and standing.

"I don't think it's the topic, cousin," he said, making his way over to the windows to stand next to Tuck. "I think it's your approach to it."

"You know I won't speak of Harrison to potential bene-factors," Tuck said almost defensively.

A line appeared between Liam's eyes. "I know, cousin. I know. What makes you think I would suggest that route of bargaining again?"

Tuck licked his lips and looked out the window. "I told Lady Eloise about Harrison."

Liam was quiet for so long Tuck was forced to turn his gaze away from the window. He found his cousin smiling a curious smile he quickly snuffed out when Tuck looked at him.

"You did?" Liam asked. "And how did she take it?"

"Graciously," Tuck said, trying very hard not to remember how she had taken his hand into hers like she meant to comfort him forever. "She will make a good duchess. I can attest to that. You've chosen well." Each word was like a razor blade slicing through his throat.

"Did she perhaps suggest what I've been suggesting? That

you tell potential benefactors of your personal reasons for your research?"

Tuck forced out the truth. "Yes."

Liam laughed, the sound light and carefree. "I thought she would. Lady Eloise seems the practical sort, don't you think? She'd probably be a good expedition companion." Liam paused, his head titling as he thought. "Can you imagine her facing down a polar bear? I should think the polar bear would run for its life."

Tuck stared, unblinking at his cousin. "Lady Eloise cannot go on expedition. She's a lady."

Liam frowned. "A lady? Were you not there when she was thrown into the lake by that dog? She acted as though it were nothing more taxing than having to compile a menu for a dinner." Liam shook his head. "She may be better at expeditions than you, cousin."

Tuck digested this, trying to pair his feelings for Eloise with the image his cousin conjured with his words. When Tuck thought of Eloise, he saw a woman he very much desired, one he wanted in a way he'd never felt before, a woman with whom he thought he could build a life. But what Liam was suggesting was a...partner.

"I suppose we shall never find out," Tuck said.

That curious expression Tuck had witnessed of late appeared on Liam's face again, but his cousin spoke before Tuck could question it. "What did Lady Eloise have to say of Harrison's death?"

Tuck looked back out the window. "Much the same as you have said. That I wouldn't be bartering Harrison's memory. That I would be ensuring his death wasn't meaningless."

Tuck could feel Liam nod beside him. "She's intelligent too. Hmm." He paused, and Tuck knew the next sentence would be self-congratulatory. "I am an incredible judge of character."

Tuck turned, a smile already on his lips at knowing his cousin so well, but the smile vanished as soon as he saw the look of confusion on Liam's face.

"What is it now?"

Liam shook his head. "I'm not sure it's important, but it's something that's bothered me since you first told me of your idea to launch an expedition to the northern climes."

Tuck straightened. "If you think to dissuade me, we've been over this. Spitsbergen is not hostile as long as one prepares properly. Even now there is talk of holiday tours traveling there. It's not like—"

Liam held up a hand, cutting him off. "It's not the location that bothers me, but rather how you speak of the expedition itself. You make it sound as though you plan to conduct this endeavor on your own."

Tuck shifted from one foot to the other, suddenly uncomfortable by his cousin's probing. The thing was Liam was a good judge of character, and he was also insightful, analyzing a situation in a deeper and more complex way than Tuck would. It was why Tuck had accepted his help in coming to London in the first place. He knew Liam would be a good ally in his quest for a benefactor. He just hadn't expected his scrutiny to be so acute.

Liam went on. "You might hear of explorers going it alone, but the truth of the matter is they always have a team with them. Particularly a partner they can rely on. Livingstone had Oswell. Burton had Speke. Who will you have, Tuck?"

Tuck felt the unsettling feeling dissipate. "I'm not an explorer. I'm a scientist. They are hardly the same thing."

Liam shook his head. "That's merely semantics, cousin. I

think you know that." His tone was soft and careful, unlike his usual jovial nature, and Tuck felt the weight of it.

Liam was right. Calling himself by another title didn't make the situation any different. He was headed into an extreme climate in a hostile terrain. He would be foolish to attempt it alone. And yet, he had always thought of this expedition as something he must do alone, for Harrison.

"I suppose I hadn't thought of it in those terms. Of course I'll have the usual support team with me. Porters and the like."

"And will you speak to your porters about the doubts that haunt you when the darkness comes?" Liam asked, stilling Tuck in his nervous shifting. "I've heard tales that the sun sets that far north for months at a time. How will you cope with such darkness? Will your porters comfort you? Assure you everything will be all right?"

"I will remind myself that the sun will rise again." He tried for a smile, but Liam wasn't joking. Tuck sobered. "I realize you have a point, cousin, but I'm not sure I have the luxury of indulging such thinking. I don't even have a benefactor as of yet, let alone a partner."

A strange thing occurred then. It was like a mirage unraveling before his eyes. When he spoke the word *partner*, his brain conjured the image of Eloise that night in the courtyard, her head tilted to the sky. He swallowed and forced the thought away. He'd seen the look on her face that day on the lakeshore. The envy that was clearly writ on her face as she surveyed the duchess and her brood. Eloise would have that. With Liam.

Liam's face opened finally, and Tuck felt the weight of his cousin's scrutiny lift. For now.

"Well then, we should see about remedying that. Today, in fact." Liam clapped his hands together as if a decision had been made and turned toward the door. "I'd like to take a ride in the park before we leave. If you don't mind, I shall leave you to push your sausage around your plate on your own."

"Leave?" Tuck called after Liam before his cousin could escape. "Where exactly are we to be going?"

Liam turned, that full smile once more on his face. "To a garden party."

* * *

"Eloise, we are all well aware of your delightful personality, but I would find it much more enjoyable if you were to refrain from entering any bodies of water whilst we attend the Brocklehurst garden party." Her mother arched a single reddish-brown eyebrow. "Do you think that is something you might achieve?"

Eloise sat across from her mother in the Stoke Bruerne carriage while they made their way the short distance to the Brocklehurst home. A dip in the road rocked the carriage enough to have Eloise's shoulder going into Annie's who sat beside her. She glanced at her sister to find the woman attempting to hold back a smile.

Eloise looked properly at her sister. She hadn't seen Annie so animated in…well, more than a year. Perhaps even longer than that. A spark of curiosity wavered inside of her, but she had no time to reflect on it as Annie spoke.

"Really Mother, you mustn't think of it like that. I think the Duke of Ardley was only too happy to sweep in and save Eloise from herself. You know how men like to think we need their protection." Annie stopped trying to hide her smile, and it was clearly visible now as she faced Eloise. "I think Eloise has rather endeared herself to the man. We should expect a proposal within the month, I should think."

Their mother sat up. "Do you really think so? I would

have thought drowning oneself in the Serpentine was off putting."

"Do you know I'm sitting right here?" Eloise said, looking between the two of them. "And I didn't need rescuing," she added with a mutter.

Heat came to her cheeks so unexpectedly she looked out the window to hide her face. She remembered Tuck's arms around her as he settled his coat on her shoulders, the way he'd held on just a little too long, how she'd wanted him to keep holding her.

And then later…in the courtyard…

"Well be that as it may, I think it would be best to present yourself in a more favorable manor this afternoon. You don't want to be getting a reputation, do you?" Her mother's eyebrows crept together accusatorially.

Eloise had looked back at her mother when she'd begun to speak, but at this, Eloise looked away again, the heat climbing up her neck.

If only her mother knew what *kind* of reputation Eloise was in danger of acquiring.

Really, she must stop *kissing* the man. Why did she do that? It seemed whenever they were alone she couldn't stop herself from…from…from assaulting him. That night in the courtyard had clearly been her doing. She had touched him first.

But he hadn't stopped her.

God, the way he had lifted her, pinned her against that tree, *licked* her—

"Eloise, are you all right? You look like you're about to be sick." Her mother's voice was pitched with concern. "You know Lady Heyworth told me Rosemary is already talking about you, and it's not in favorable terms. You're not going to embarrass me again today, are you?"

Rosemary Hayes-Martin, Viscountess Bowes, was Eloise's

mother's arch nemesis. Eloise wished that were an exaggeration, but sadly, it was not. Nancy and Viscountess Bowes had been competing against each other for some unknown prize since Eloise could remember. The current situation on the Marriage Mart only intensified the rivalry.

Eloise tugged at the high collar of her gown. "It's just this incessant rocking. I'm afraid I didn't eat much before we left, and my stomach is quite sensitive, you know."

"Your stomach is perfectly fine," Annie said beside her.

Eloise glared.

Annie had caught Eloise returning to the library after her midnight rendezvous in the courtyard with Tuck, and the incident had likely sprouted some suspicion Annie would never overtly poke but would take great pleasure in teasing. Eloise communicated her annoyance with her eyes, but Annie only smiled that soft smile she had when she knew exactly how uncomfortable she was making her little sister.

If only Gwen was here.

Not for the first time did she miss her older sister. Gwen would know what to do in this terrible situation. Gwen always knew what to do.

The carriage eased to a stop, and her mother shooed them out before the tiger had even opened the door.

The afternoon was lovely, and Eloise stepped from the carriage into a bath of lukewarm sunshine. She hated it immediately, raising a hand to shield her eyes from the sun even though it was hardly blinding. It was a typical English spring day, enough for comfortability but not enough to overtax one's senses, blast it. At least if the weather were troubling she'd have something else to focus on.

And not the fact that Tuck was walking into the Brocklehurst gardens a mere ten steps ahead of them, Ardley at his side.

"Oh my, I think our timing could not have been better. Eloise, you must—"

"I forgot my wrap," she squeaked, diving back into the carriage.

She sat down heavily on the bench she had just vacated, berating herself for her weakness. They had a plan. She would help him make contacts in London. He would shower Ardley with tales of her virtue. It was a plan.

So why did the very sight of him have parts of her coiling she didn't know could coil? Why did her heart start to thumping? God, were her hands shaking? This was ludicrous.

"You didn't bring a shawl." Eloise looked to the open door where Annie stood waiting, her expression bland. "Care to tell me what's really going on?"

Eloise pushed back her shoulders. "No. I do not."

Annie tilted her head. "Do you think it will offend me?"

"No," Eloise said, gathering her skirts to climb back out of the carriage. She stopped on the pavement next to her sister. "I can't tell you what is happening because it will make me look bad."

With that, she lifted her nose and left her sister standing on the pavement. She didn't miss her sister's stifled laugh, however.

The Brocklehurst's garden was teeming with the best the *ton* had to offer, and Eloise had expected no less. It bolstered her resolve, and she found herself stepping more assuredly into the orchid tent, scanning the crowd as she went. There were any number of people to whom she could introduce Tuck. It seemed this plan had a far greater chance of working.

Especially because when she stepped from the tent she ran nearly directly into both the Duke of Grimsby and Tuck himself.

"Lady Eloise," Grimsby said.

She stopped short, heard Grimsby's greeting, but her eyes went immediately to Tuck. She forced herself to think, a smile coming to her lips more from practice than actual thought.

"Your Grace, what a pleasure to see you. I trust you are well." She turned to Tuck, prayed her expression didn't change. "Mr. Ryan, very nice to see you again."

"It's an honor, Lady Eloise." Tuck bowed then of all things.

She wanted to look at Grimsby. Could he sense the awkwardness in that very moment?

"Lady Eloise, is your sister in attendance? I should like to ask after her wellbeing."

It was a moment before she registered what Grimsby was saying. "Annie? Oh yes, of course. You'll probably find her in the Brocklehurst library." She couldn't stop the frown her words conjured. The library? God, she was nearly declaring the truth right there. Telling Grimsby exactly how Annie had caught her in the midst of her scandalous rendezvous. "She's spending an awful lot of time in libraries lately. Perhaps she's facing a slump in her reading material and is looking for inspiration." The lie rolled easily from her lips. She had no idea why Annie was in the library that night. She only knew it had nearly exposed her.

"The library?"

She nodded. "Yes, quite. I've heard the Brocklehurst library is extensive. More than likely that's where she's wandered off to." After Eloise had left her standing on the pavement, but she didn't say that bit.

"Thank you, Lady Eloise. Tuck, I assume you're confident in your next steps with Renshaw?"

At the name, it was like a fog lifted from her brain. "The Earl of Renshaw?" She looked to Tuck. "Do you need to speak with the man? I'd be happy to provide an introduction. He's a dear old friend of my grandmother Bitsy's." It took everything in her to keep her tone neutral, keep her eyes from changing, prevent any hint that she and Tuck had discussed this very thing in a courtyard at midnight.

"An introduction?" Did Tuck's voice wobble just the smallest bit?

She eyed him, willing him to keep it together for just a little longer, and in doing so, caught sight of the man in question sitting on a bench behind Tuck. "Grandmother Bitsy is with him right now. Let us go over, and I'll introduce you."

She moved before Tuck could respond, and he was forced to follow or snub her in the middle of a packed social event. He followed as she'd expected him to. Carefully she glanced back to see Grimsby had moved on toward the house.

"This is exactly what we talked about," she said, keeping her voice low. "I help you, and you help me."

When his eyes met hers, they were full of heat, and she remembered what they had been doing the last time they'd spoken those words. She swallowed and looked straight ahead.

"Grandmother," she said when they reached the bench where Grandmother Bitsy and the Earl of Renshaw were seated. "Grandmother, you've met the Honorable Mr. Tucker Ryan, but I had hoped to introduce him to your friend."

Grandmother Bitsy looked up, blinking. "Is that you, Nancy?"

Eloise shifted so she blocked the sun from her grandmother's eyes.

Her grandmother's expression relaxed as she smiled in recognition. "Oh, Tippy, darling, this is my youngest granddaughter. She's the one I was telling you about. The one who is always getting into trouble."

"Grandmother." Eloise hadn't meant to speak the word so

harshly. It was simply a reaction to her grandmother's rather unfair accusation. "I don't *always* get in trouble," Eloise added softly.

Her grandmother laughed and placed a hand on the earl's arm. It was such a casual gesture but one which spoke volumes, and Eloise wondered just how good a friend the earl was. "You see, Tippy, dear. She wouldn't be so quick to defend herself if she didn't know it were true."

The earl laughed now, his head going back as he did so. The sunlight caught his face, and she was able to see him properly. He was somewhere around her grandmother's age with a nearly bald head rimmed by tufts of gray hair. More hair came out of his ears and poked in odd angles from his eyebrows than he had on his head. He had an overlarge nose with a slight bend at the end that made his face look more like a caricature than an actual face, and she found herself drawn to it. He was clean-shaven and smelled of something herbal like basil. Nothing fancy, which matched his attire. His clothes were several years out of date but well-kept as if the latest fashions mattered little to him. Or perhaps it was simply because the rumors about Renshaw were true. The man was utterly broke. Still, he was a good connection for Tuck to have.

He patted Grandmother Bitsy's hand. "Oh Bitty, dear, you mustn't convince me. A granddaughter of yours is sure to carry your penchant for the daring."

Eloise looked between Renshaw and her grandmother, her curiosity stoked. The woman had married at eighteen, had one son before her husband died before the age of thirty, and she'd spent much of her life a happy and wealthy widow. She had spent the rest of her years doing exactly as she pleased. Eloise knew some of her grandmother's stories, but the earl's comment left her wondering just how much she didn't know.

She let their laughter die out before speaking again. "Grandmother, about my friend. I had hoped—"

Grandmother Bitsy waved her off. "Oh yes, yes, child. I heard you." She turned to Renshaw. "Tippy, dear, this man is my Eloise's friend, the one I told you about. He's the man my granddaughter is going to marry."

CHAPTER 7

For a split second, Tuck thought it might be true.

For a solitary moment, he believed he was marrying Eloise, that the heavy weight of betrayal he'd been carrying around for weeks now was unwarranted, and he was free to love the woman he loved.

Loved?

He glanced swiftly at Eloise to find her mouth hanging open, her eyes wide as she stared at her grandmother. Did he love her? It was too soon, wasn't it? He'd only just met her. How could something as weighty and important as love grow in such a small time?

It was at that horrible moment he recalled Liam's words from earlier that day, about Tuck embarking on his expedition alone. As he studied Eloise, he couldn't help but wonder.

Was she capable of being his partner in such extreme circumstances?

It was ludicrous, of course. He had meant it when he'd told Liam she was a lady, and ladies did not embark on expeditions. But what if?

He was rattled from his thoughts when Eloise spoke

sternly. "Grandmother. You know perfectly well I have not accepted anyone's proposal. Most certainly not Mr. Ryan's."

She needn't be quite *that* stern about it, need she?

"Mr. Ryan is the cousin of the Duke of Ardley and dear friend of our family. You know as much."

Dear friend? God, he was a friend now? This afternoon could not get much worse.

But it did. Of course, it did. Grandmother Bitsy looked at him when she said, "I didn't say anything about a proposal, dearie. I said you were going to marry this gentleman." Here she pointed directly at Tuck. "What does a proposal have to do with that?"

Eloise blinked, but Renshaw chuckled softly, the movement upsetting the hat he had cradled on his lap.

"Oh Bitty, you do know how to put a point on things." Renshaw looked up, his eyes squinting rather a lot for the amount of sun they were in. "So you're the chap my Bitty has been talking about. I hear you're a man of science."

Tuck glanced at Eloise, but she was still shooting daggers at her grandmother with her eyes. He looked back at Renshaw, not quite believing it could be this simple. He'd spent the last few weeks climbing every obstacle he encountered when it came to speaking to potential benefactors, and he was fairly certain he had nearly reached pariah status amongst the *ton*. Renshaw's overture seemed almost like a trap for how easily it came.

"Yes," he started hesitantly. "My field of study is the aurora borealis. The northern lights. I wish to discover the effect of solar storms on our modern-day communication systems."

Renshaw's eyes squinted even more as he smiled. "Is that so? Tell me, young man. Do you plan to travel in your research?"

This was most definitely a trap, but Eloise had begun to

whisper argue with her grandmother, so he couldn't look to her for help.

"I do, in fact," he went on. "I'm currently seeking to launch an expedition to Spitsbergen. It's an ideal location for studying the aurora."

Renshaw tapped his hat against his thighs. "I'll say. What a splendid notion." He held up a hand, pointing one finger into the air. "Do you know I used to travel a great deal? There's nothing like it. Setting off to unknown places." The man's exuberance in speaking gave him the slightest speech impediment. Almost as though he were so eager to get the words out that they became jammed against his front teeth. "Do you know what my favorite journey was?"

Something inside of Tuck began to rise on a bubble of hope. Although Grimsby had indicated Renshaw had no funds and likely couldn't support a research expedition, Tuck might find in the older gentleman an ally, one who thrived on discovery and exploration.

"What was it?" Tuck asked, urging the man on.

Renshaw snapped his fingers in the air. "Cornwall," he said triumphantly, and the bubble of hope inside of Tuck popped. "There's nothing more beautiful than the Cornwall coast." But then Renshaw's expression began to fade, and his hand sank back to his lap. "Although I don't travel so much anymore. Not since I lost my Carolina."

Tuck took a seat on the bench next to Renshaw, so the man wasn't forced to keep looking up at him. "Was that your wife?" Tuck asked now, concern pooling.

Renshaw's forlorn expression cracked a little. "Oh yes, she was. My beautiful Carolina. She always traveled with me. The best travel companion a man could ask for." He slapped his thigh with his hat once more. "Tell me, young man. Do you have a companion to go with you on this journey you have planned?" He nodded in Eloise's direction, and Tuck saw she had bent over and was whispering in her grandmother's ear. He caught the words *polite* and *company* and tried not to smile. "I understand Lady Eloise is quite a formidable lady. Perhaps she would make a good partner."

Why was everyone going on about Lady Eloise and expeditions?

Tuck laughed to ease the tension he was beginning to feel in his shoulders. "Lady Eloise is courting my cousin, the Duke of Ardley. I'm afraid there's been some kind of misunderstanding in regard to our relationship."

"She's attached to the Duke of Ardley?" Renshaw asked. "Then why is she here with you?"

Nothing had struck Tuck more than that simple question. He swallowed. "Lady Eloise is doing me a kindness in aiding me with introductions. I'm new to all of this, you see. I'm a professor in Oxford, so I don't often have a chance to frequent London society."

Renshaw's face opened. "Ah, that I can understand only too well. My Carolina was much the same. Always helping where she was able. I can see similar traits in young Lady Eloise. Is there a particular introduction you're interested in, young man?" He screwed up his mouth to one side and leaned closer conspiratorially. "I've been in this world long enough to know that one's connections can mean everything. So tell me, who is it you wish to meet?"

Tuck couldn't stop a smile at the older man's good nature. "I'm afraid it's the worst kind. The ones with money to spare."

Renshaw straightened with a hearty laugh. "Oh, my young man, you are right. Those are the worst kind. And what is the intended use for this money?"

Tuck looked down at his feet, the familiar feeling of unease creeping over him as he talked about his work in relation to needing money. "I need funding for the expedition I plan to launch in the fall."

"Ah, I see. To study the aurora as you mentioned." Renshaw leaned back, his hat tapping a staccato against his thigh. "I'll say, who have you approached already?" The earl's gaze traveled around the cluster of guests in front of them. "I should think Stockwell is a good prospect. Made heaps of money last year in iron." He tilted his head toward Tuck and dropped his voice. "Better get on it soon though. His wife has a wee problem with baubles. She'll spend through Stockwell's earnings before the end of the season. Mark my words." He straightened again. "There's Hanratty and Beauclair, of course. Those are the usual suspects. I would stay away from Burdette though."

"Is the man unscrupulous?" Tuck inquired.

"No," Renshaw said pleasantly. "He just has a predilection for a pipe tobacco that smells far too much like rotten onions. It's exceedingly uncomfortable to be around the man."

Tuck smiled now and eased back on the bench. Grimsby was right in suggesting he speak to Renshaw. The man was proving to be a delight, and Tuck could already feel his confidence growing.

"I think I should like to know more about you, my lord. If you don't mind."

Renshaw started at this, straightening so quickly his hat nearly fell off his lap. "Me?" he asked, the incredulity clear in his voice. "Everyone knows I'm not more than an old totter. What can you gain from spending time with me? I've nothing to offer."

"Come now," Tuck said. "You mustn't say such things. I've enjoyed the last few minutes with you more than I have the entire time I've been in London. That's not nothing."

Renshaw's smile deepened. "You're a bright young man. I

could tell that straightaway. Lady Eloise would be so lucky to have you for a husband."

Tuck felt the razor blade of guilt slash at him, but he was saved from speaking when Liam himself arrived. Tuck got to his feet as his cousin approached.

"Renshaw!" Liam called from several steps away. "It's been too long." He shook the earl's hand heartily. "I see you've met my cousin here."

"We've been having a wonderful chat, Ardley. It's a shame you haven't invited your cousin to London sooner." Renshaw placed the hat on top of his head and stood. "Mr. Ryan, I hope you meant what you said just now. Call on me anytime. Bitty knows the address."

With that the earl ambled away, greeting people as he went with a nod and a kind word. Tuck watched him go.

"The Earl of Renshaw?" Liam said softly beside him. "The man is an old totter."

"I think I rather like old totters."

Liam eyed him. "You're very strange sometimes."

Tuck frowned. "You've mentioned that before. What do you want?"

Liam pressed a hand innocently to his chest. "Why would you think I'm in need of something from you?"

"You have that earnest look in your eye."

Liam dropped his hand. "I don't care for how observant you are."

Tuck didn't say anything. He merely glared at his cousin.

Liam's gaze shifted ever so slightly to where Eloise had taken the seat Renshaw had vacated and was working to straighten her grandmother's shawl, which seemed to have become entangled in the yew hedge behind her. "I need you to escort Lady Eloise for me."

"No." The single word shot from Tuck's lips so quickly he wasn't sure who was more surprised.

Liam veered back ever so slightly and cast a quick glance over his shoulder. "I promised old Hollinrake I would take his daughter for a turn about the garden to show her off. He's trying to find her a match this season, and you know how disadvantaged she is. Having her be seen with me will do the girl wonders."

Tuck knew what Liam wasn't saying. Even though he'd been in London only a few weeks, Tuck had met Hollinrake's daughter. She was a wallflower to put it politely and rather unfortunate of face to put it not so politely. Being seen with Liam really would be a boon for her.

"What has that got to do with Lady Eloise?" He kept his tone low even though Eloise was preoccupied and several feet away from them.

"I don't wish to waste the entire afternoon. I need a wife this season, and I can't possibly choose one if I don't talk to the lady I'm supposed to be courting." He gestured with his head toward the garden beyond. "Take her for a turn about the rose beds, and I'll meet you by the fountain at the back of the gardens. You'll take the Hollinrake girl back to her father, and I'll get a chance to speak to Lady Eloise."

Tuck cared for this idea not at all, but his cousin was making a kind gesture for a rather unfortunate girl. "Fine. But this is the last time I help you with Lady Eloise. You know perfectly well what a fine wife she'd make." He didn't realize that was what he meant to say, and Liam's expression mirrored the shock Tuck felt.

"I see. If she's so lovely, why don't you marry her?"

Tuck didn't answer. He waved Liam off and stepped over to Eloise. "Lady Eloise?" He interrupted what sounded like an argument about the merits of pantaloons. "I was wondering if you'd enjoy a turn about the gardens." Her eyes narrowed in question. "My cousin suggested you might like to take in the rose beds."

Her eyes widened at the mention of Liam, and she patted her grandmother's arm. "Grandmother, will you be all right if I go with Mr. Ryan?"

Grandmother Bitsy's attention was already elsewhere though, and her reply was little more than a murmur of parting.

Eloise stood and took his arm. He led her in the direction of the rose garden.

"Liam would like to meet us at the fountain at the rear of the garden. He wishes to speak with you."

"And did you remember to speak well of me to him?" Her voice was playful, and painfully, he recalled their bargain.

"Yes," he said. "Something like that."

He steered her around the yew hedge that separated them from the rose garden and tried very hard not to think about Liam's suggestion of making Eloise his wife.

* * *

"I must apologize for my grandmother," Eloise said as soon as they were out of earshot of the other guests, slipping between the yew hedges that would lead them to the rose beds.

Tuck was quiet for too long, and she risked a glance in his direction. He was staring straight ahead, his eyes vacant, and she wondered what was occupying his thoughts.

She went on. "My grandmother has a fanciful notion of what she wishes for her granddaughters, and I'm afraid it sometimes colors her speech." He still didn't say anything, and she felt the rush of words as if she could drown the uncomfortable silence. "My grandfather died quite young, you see, and my grandmother was left to her own devices, my grandfather having left her in good financial standing to see her through. She lived a grand life, although you wouldn't know it now. She traveled all over the Continent and would have gone to America if the tides had been right." She laughed then, recalling her grandmother's favorite story of being thwarted in her adventures by Poseidon. "She studied at the Louvre, sketched at the Pantheon, all while taking my father in tow." She looked again at Tuck, unable to stop her story. "She once danced with a prince. She said she would have run away with him if he'd asked, but he never did, and she held too much respect for herself to chase after him."

Tuck's expression was almost grave, and it had the story dying out on her lips. They walked on for several paces before she could no longer take his silence.

"Tuck, what is it? Has my grandmother upset you so?" She swallowed, dared to speak the thing that had plagued her for days now. "Is this about that night in the courtyard? Do you regret it?"

She didn't know if she could bear his answer. What if he did regret it?

He stopped so abruptly he nearly tore her arm from her shoulder. She turned to face him, and she stilled, taking in his face. There was a fierceness there she'd never seen before, and it stole her breath. She realized absently that they had wandered far from the other guests, their incessant chatter almost gone from her ears, replaced with the sound of the breeze stirring the yew hedges about her and the occasional call of a sparrow.

"Tuck, what's..." But she couldn't finish the sentence because his eyes had changed, deepening with something she couldn't name.

They were alone again. Somehow, after all they had determined not to, they were alone. Never had it been more dangerous for two people to be alone, and she glanced from one side to the other, willing someone to come down the path they were on, someone to discover them, someone to stop her from making another mistake.

But no one came, and Tuck still held her arm.

"What do you want, Eloise?" he said, his voice unlike the one she knew. It was lower, softer, more intense, as though her answer might determine whether he lived or died. "What do you really want?"

He had been holding her arm, but he moved now, slipping his hand down to take hers. He tugged her toward him, and she was helpless to resist him. She fell into his arms, her hands going to press against his chest as he released her arm to take hold of her hips.

"What do you *really* want?" He stared into her eyes, and she thought she might be caught there forever, in the wonder and possibility she saw in his gaze. "Not what society wants, not what your mother wants, not what's expected of you. What do you want, Eloise Bounds?"

She felt it, the thing she had pushed down, the thing she had given up, the thing she had thought she had discarded, but she hadn't. She knew that now because it pressed against her insides. It couldn't be held in, not when he looked at her like that, not when he held her like this.

Not when he demanded of her the one thing she couldn't give.

But to him she did give it. They were alone there, surrounded by the tall hedges that blocked them from the rest of it. Right now she could answer his question because society wasn't there, her mother wasn't there, the expectations they held for her weren't there. It was only she and Tuck and this thing that had so inexplicably arisen between them.

This.

This was what she wanted. This was what she had always wanted. She had waited so long to find it, but it had been forced from her dreams when the reality of a third season and the prospect of marrying a duke had proven to be greater than her own wishes. But it didn't mean her wishes went away.

They were still there, and his words called to them, summoning up the thing inside of her she had tried so desperately to hide.

"I want love." The words slipped through her lips so easily.

She gave it to him, her secret, and somehow she knew he wouldn't use it to hurt her. Not intentionally.

He didn't say anything, but he didn't have to. His fingers flexed, digging into her hips, claiming her in ways words couldn't, and it pierced her heart. Why now? Why this man? Could the world be so cruel?

"Love." The word wasn't a question, nor did he seem to be mocking her. It was more that he was trying to figure out the word by shaping it with his mouth. He laughed then, a horrible, sad sound that made her heart shudder. "Love. What a treacherous word, Eloise. It's gotten people into all kinds of trouble." He removed his hands from her hips, and the softest of sighs escaped her lips uncontrollably. He cupped her face, tilted her head back until he could rest his forehead against hers. "And I suppose you want children too? Don't you? A whole brood of them." He paused, but she didn't think she was meant to answer him. His chest rose and fell under her hands as though he were holding something in that was too big for him, too big for anyone to contain. "You want a husband you can wrap around your precious little finger, a biddable sop who will do whatever your heart desires. Isn't that what you want?" His voice had grown hard, and she wondered if he meant to hurt her with his words.

Well, it wouldn't work, not with her, because in his voice

she could hear the lies he was telling. Not to her, but to himself.

She pulled herself from his grasp so quickly his hands hung suspended in the air the way they had that day in the drawing room so long ago. "No, that's not what I want." She was surprised at how steady her voice was, how sure, when she felt anything but confident just then. It was truth that drove her words and nothing else. "I want love, Tuck. Actual love. Not the kind of thing a person would use as a weapon against another person." She straightened her shoulders and took a step toward him as if by being closer he might understand her better. "I want the kind of love where my husband wants to do those things not because I manipulate him, but because if he doesn't, his heart just won't be right." She flung her arms wide. "I want a whole house full of children. Children bring laughter and noise and—" She shook her head and wrinkled her nose. "And mucus sometimes." She looked him directly in the eye. "Sometimes they bring so much mucus, but children mean the future and hope and a continuation of the love I will share with my husband. That's what I want, Tuck." She prodded him in the chest. "I thought you might understand something of that, but clearly you do not."

He surprised her by taking her by the finger she used to poke him and wrench her hand aside until she was once more standing flush against his body.

"Do you think I don't know of what you speak, Eloise? Do you think I haven't been trying to stop that very thing from happening between us for more than a month?"

She studied his eyes, mesmerized by them as they lit with a fury and passion she'd never witnessed in him before.

"Because if you think I haven't, then you are not feeling what I'm feeling, and I've been a fool this whole time."

She grabbed the front of his jacket, wrapping her fingers into his lapels as if she might rip the garment from his body.

"Of course I've been feeling that, you infuriating man. Why else would I put myself through such torture? A mere glimpse of you is all I need to feed my soul a little longer until it's inevitably crushed when we must part. Why would I subject myself to such torment if it were for anything less than sustenance?"

It was as though something insurmountable shimmered between them. Perhaps it was all that stood against them, all that kept them apart, but just then it didn't seem such a challenge. It seemed fragile and weak and all so very human, and it broke her in a way nothing else could.

This was what she had wanted all along. To care for another so much as to cause herself pain in order to save him. Save him from having to betray someone who meant so very much to him.

"Sustenance?" He repeated the word as if it shocked him. "If sustenance is what you want then you shall have it."

His mouth closed on hers before she could anticipate it, and the force of his kiss rocked her back on her heels, but he caught her in his arms, cradling her preciously in such opposition to the heat of his kiss. Her body warred from one extreme to the other as he continued to ravage her, his mouth doing wicked work along her jawline to the sensitive spot behind her ear before sucking her earlobe into his mouth.

The cry lodged in her throat as her body wound impossibly fast to an impossibly tight spiral until she knew she would shatter. But he wasn't done. He followed the line of her neck down, tilting her back in his arms as his teeth scraped her collarbone and then lower until his lips touched the edge of her bodice.

Suddenly she wanted him to touch her, there, now. Never before had her desire been so persistent. Perhaps it was him. Perhaps it was the despair of knowing she would never have him. Perhaps it was simply the threat of being caught. Whatever it was, her core pulsed with need for him, and she let him take.

But he didn't.

When his lips would have gone farther, he stopped, drawing back so quickly she stumbled against the hedge at her back, clinging to its branches to keep from falling. She blinked until he came into focus, and she hated how even now, when he'd rejected her, she longed to be once more in his arms.

"If Liam wishes, he can find you himself." And with that, Tuck strode away.

CHAPTER 8

It had started to rain by the time Tuck reached 14
Grosvenor Square.

He hadn't planned on visiting Renshaw quite so soon, but
after that afternoon in the Brocklehurst garden, he'd been
unsettled. He couldn't focus on anything. Not his expedition,
not his research, and not even his quest to find a funder. His
brain was like a butterfly, flitting from one shrub to the next,
never staying long enough for any permanence. He'd spent
an entire week in a fog, and he no longer knew what day
it was.

The only thing that held his attention for any length of
time was Eloise, and then it was only in pieces. The touch of
her bare skin beneath his fingertips, the smell of her hair
when he'd nibbled her earlobe, the feel of her hips in his
hands.

Eloise.

He stared at 14 Grosvenor Square as if it held answers,
but it was only a stone facade now speckled with dark spots
as the spitting mist turned to rain. He forced himself up the
stairs and found the door opening under his knock. He gave

his card to the butler and waited, turning up his collar as the servant went to see if Renshaw was at home.

He stared at his feet, at the door, and at the street behind him, feeling a degree of uncertainty he'd never felt before in his life.

He was a man of science. He'd always known the next step, the next hypothesis, the next experiment. But now, he didn't know what to do.

Eloise was one thing, but he couldn't lay all the blame at her feet. When he'd come to London, his objective had been clear. Find a benefactor to fund his expedition to Spitsbergen to continue his research into the aurora borealis.

But now this intention seemed almost foolish and worse, alarmingly naive.

Liam was right. Was Tuck really expecting to make such a journey alone? He hadn't given it a thought, but he couldn't ignore his cousin's warning. Simply surviving on Spitsbergen would be a challenge. He would bring the required equipment, of course, and guides experienced with the harsh climate. But as inexperienced as Tuck was with such extreme travel, even he knew it would test his limits.

And what would he do then? Confide in his sled dogs?

Or was he simply allowing his determination to be swayed? The expedition he wished to undertake would be no holiday to the sunny shores of Italy. It would be grueling at the best of times. But would it be unbearable? Would it be enough to drive him in search of companionship?

He'd always had Liam to lean on. His parents had been attentive and kind, but they were not a demonstrative family, and *feelings* was not a word spoken in his childhood home. Whenever Tuck had truly struggled with something, he'd always gone to Harrison. The gap in years between them had leant an air of sophistication to his older brother that had given Tuck comfort. Harrison would know what to do. Tuck only wished his brother were here so he could ask him.

Tuck was contemplating the buttons of his coat when the door opened again, and the bland-faced butler informed Tuck that Renshaw was at home.

It was relief to be out of the rain, and Tuck took a moment to take in the small foyer into which the butler had shown him. While shedding his dripping coat and hat, he noticed the space was heavily accented in wooden motifs from the paneling to the intricate trim framing the doors.

He had just handed his gloves to the butler when his eyes fell on something that seemed out of place. It was a small wooden carving of a woman kneeling and holding her extended belly. He'd once had cause to collaborate with an anthropology colleague, and Tuck was fairly certain a similar wooden figurine had been in the man's office.

But why would the Earl of Renshaw who claimed his most favorite trip had been to the Cornwall coast have an Incan Pachamama statue on a table in his foyer?

Tuck was pulled from his thoughts when the butler gestured for Tuck to follow him. The man led Tuck farther into the house along a central corridor that was fashioned with the same dark paneling as the foyer. Distantly he heard the sounds of a house being attended to by servants, the shifting of cutlery as though silver were being polished and the distinct thwap of curtains being dusted.

When the butler turned into a room off the corridor, Tuck was momentarily concerned the servant had brought him to the wrong place. This was not a public room meant for receiving guests. The moderate-sized room was littered with evidence of a person's existence from a pile of discarded newspapers to a stack of plates, the remnants of a meal evident on their surfaces. Half-empty teacups covered half the low table set between sofas, and a stack of books had toppled over on the floor beneath it.

Over the sound of the rain, Tuck heard the crackle of a fire and turned to find an inglenook fireplace held a small blaze and before it was a chair in which Renshaw himself sat.

Except—

It was only his mother's persistence in teaching her children good manners that Tuck didn't show his shock on his face when he took in the sight of Renshaw sprawled before the fire. Because the earl was, indeed, sprawled.

The older man wore a dressing gown that was approximately two sizes too big, rolled at the cuffs several times, and with elbows worn so thin it was as though the threads of the fabric were held together by mere suggestion. Underneath this, Tuck saw the folds of a nightshirt which ended just above a pair of socks that had melted down around the earl's ankles and finally finished with a pair of slippers.

Renshaw stood, his arms going wide in greeting, which drew apart the panels of the dressing gown to reveal the tea-spotted nightshirt Tuck had glimpsed along the gown's hem. "You came to visit an old totter, I see! A man of adventure. I knew it at once. Welcome, young Ryan." He gestured for Tuck to join him before the fire in the opposite chair, and it was a second before Tuck remembered how to move his legs.

"Renshaw," Tuck said by way of greeting, but the earl waved him off.

"The name is Tippy. I never very much liked anyone who called me Renshaw, and I like you. So please, Tippy."

Tuck nodded and took the seat the older man indicated.

"Now then," Tippy said, resuming his own seat.

Tuck steeled himself, wondering if the man would cross his legs out of habit, but thankfully he didn't, settling for placing his feet flat on the floor. Tuck relaxed, drawing in a much-needed breath at having been spared seeing quite so much of the earl. "What has brought you to my doorstep? Have you heard tales of my cunning exploits and come to see for yourself whether or not it's true?"

"I'm afraid the only thing I've heard of you or your reputation is what you have said yourself. That you're an old totter."

Tippy barked a laugh and clapped his hands together. "I shall sleep well tonight knowing my reputation is intact." He waved a fist in triumph before settling back into his chair. "Regan, a tea cart is in order I should think."

Tuck gave a start, not having realized the butler still stood in the door. The servant gave a bow in acknowledgment and slipped out the door.

"Well, if it's not tales of my daring escapades, then what has brought you here?"

Tuck looked back at the earl, resolve forming in his gut. "I'm afraid I'm at a crossroads in my life, and I haven't the slightest idea which way I should go. The other day at the garden party you struck me as a man of many experiences, and I suppose I have come to you for advice."

It wasn't until his face grew serious that Tuck realized the earl smiled a great deal. Tuck felt a modicum of guilt that he should affect the man's expression so.

"A crossroads, you say?" He made a snuffling noise of understanding. "It was many a time that I stood at a crossroads myself, young man. What is it you face? Is it a business conundrum or a personal one?" He clapped both hands on the armrests of his chair, curling his fingers tightly about them. "Heavens above, do not say it is a crossroads of love."

Tuck felt the earl's words like a spear to the chest. "I think it might be a professional crossroads that has been muddied by love."

Tippy squinted even more than he usually did. "Love has befuddled your plans, hasn't it?" He slapped an armrest now with the open palm of one hand. "The same thing has happened to me, I must say." He pointed a finger at Tuck. "Do you know I almost became the Prince of Hanover over a misunderstanding about a pretzel?" He shook his head. "And that was only on my Grand Tour. It was quite a way to start one's life, don't you think?" He pushed himself up in his chair. "Now tell me about your crossroads, Ryan."

"Please call me Tuck."

"Tuck? Why that's the name of an explorer. I thought you were a man of science."

Tuck couldn't help but smile. "I am a man of science."

"Does this muddied crossroad change that at all?" Tippy asked, swirling his finger in front of him as if to indicate the confusion of the situation.

"I don't think anything will change that," Tuck said, feeling the sincerity of his words.

"Ah," Tippy said, sitting back. "A man of resolve. I like that. Go on."

"You are aware of my intention to launch a research expedition to Spitsbergen to research the aurora borealis."

Tippy gave a nod.

"I came to London to find a benefactor for the expedition, and instead I'm afraid I fell in love."

Tippy's smile was slow with some kind of self-satisfaction but even worse his eyes glinted with knowing. "Isn't it a terrible thing the way love can surprise a person? Does the lady feel the same in return?"

Unbidden came the echo of Eloise's voice that night in the courtyard when he'd touched her bare flesh.

I want you.

He swallowed. "I think it's safe to say she does."

"Then I take it the problem is not unrequited love, which leads me to believe it's something else that has muddied the crossroads."

"I cannot take a wife." He'd never before thought of marriage, so focused had he been on his goal, but hearing himself say it now felt like dodging the truth. Because it wasn't that he couldn't marry Eloise because of his work. He couldn't marry her because she was courting his cousin.

"And why not?"

The question confused Tuck so much so that he immediately said, "I beg your pardon?"

Tippy tilted his head. "Why not take a wife? You make it sound as though the feat were impossible when I can assure you it happens every day. Even to people who shouldn't be married at all." This last bit was said with a sarcastic grin.

Tuck couldn't help smiling in response even though his insides felt like they were twisted up like a length of licorice. "It isn't so much as I cannot as I should not. I'll be leaving in the fall for an inhospitable clime. It would be foolish of me, if not simply irresponsible, to take a wife on such an excursion."

"You would not leave her behind as so many explorers do?" There was something odd about the way Tippy asked the question, but Tuck was too caught up in his own thoughts to think much of the tone.

"I wouldn't think of it. Why bother marrying at all if one thinks to leave the woman behind to fend for herself? That would be more irresponsible than taking her to the Arctic regions."

Tippy extended his short legs as far as they would go, crossing them at the ankles. "Well, I see the problem then. You're thinking of all the things that could go wrong with this love of yours when instead you should be thinking of everything that can go right."

"I beg your pardon."

Instead of answering, Tippy scrambled to his feet much like a dog would after rolling on its back in the grass. He made his way over to the bookshelf along the wall, retrieved something, and returned in short order. He handed the object to Tuck.

He was surprised to find it a simple frame with—of all things—a daguerreotype encased in it. It was Tippy, although much younger and with more hair atop his head, and he was seated next to a woman who towered over him. The difference in height was accentuated by the hat she wore that contained a small bird's nest from which erupted a peacock feather. The image was slightly fuzzy, indicating the pair must have moved during its processing, and as the woman was clearly laughing in the print, Tuck surmised that to be the culprit.

Tuck looked up to find Tippy smiling fondly at the print.

He tapped the frame. "Taken in Brighton. Oh, how excited we were to find a man there with a camera." He spoke the word, clearly annunciating each syllable as though the word were unfamiliar to him. "My Carolina was the daughter of a textile merchant. Her father had made a fortune in broadcloth." Tippy laughed now, waving both hands at the frame as if to push all of the nonsense away. "My father said she was wholly unsuitable to be a countess, and I married her anyway. Ran off to Gretna Green, we did, just like they do in the novels. My father was furious, but what could he do? I was his only son, and his pride in the title was of more importance than his concern for my reputation."

Tippy turned and walked back to his chair before collapsing into it, his laughter dying on his lips. He wagged a finger at the frame Tuck still held. "Carolina saved the title, but my father was too proud to admit it. She'd learned a thing or two from her own father about business, and she advised the title of Renshaw how to invest properly. I'd be moldy and festering in a distant cousin's Cumbria estate right now if it weren't for my Carolina." His eyes changed then, and he went away somewhere, deep into his memories, and Tuck couldn't help but wish that one day he'd have the blessing of deep memories into which to escape.

Tuck tapped the frame himself now. "So you're telling me it's all right to marry for love?"

The very idea seemed whimsical, and he felt foolish speaking it aloud.

Tippy clamped both hands around the armrests of his chair and surged forward, leaning over his legs to say, "Not at all, young man. I'm saying don't be so focused on the thing you think you want when something better is standing right beside you."

Tuck had the sensation of falling even though he hadn't moved, but he was prevented from saying more when the tea cart arrived. Tuck set aside the framed daguerreotype and offered to pour.

Tippy waved a hand for him to proceed and fell back in his chair again. "Two sugars, son, and I'll tell you about the greatest adventure Carolina and I ever embarked upon."

Tuck couldn't stop a smile even as he felt the unsettled feeling grow in his stomach, the very one he had come here to banish only to find the earl's words making it burn hotter. "And where did this adventure take place?"

Tippy smiled. "In the wilds of Norfolk!" he cheered.

* * *

ELOISE WOULD BECOME A NUN.

No, that was too obvious.

She'd run away. To the Continent. No, to America. Yes, America. No one would think to look for her there surely.

But what would she do for money? Father would likely cut her off. Wouldn't he? She'd have to find another means of supporting herself. But...what? She was terrible at embroi-

117

dery, her stitches having a mind of their own it seemed. Her watercolors were dismal, and her penmanship left much to be desired. It wasn't her fault really. She didn't have the time or patience ink and blotter required, and sometimes her letters were a frightful mess. At least they were legible. Mostly.

Perhaps she could be a secretary somewhere. But for who? A company? Going into trade? Oh God, her mother would be humiliated.

"If you keep it up, darling, your thoughts will give you a migraine."

Eloise glanced over at her grandmother who sat in the chair opposite, clicking knitting needles together although Eloise hadn't seen the woman complete a single stitch in the half hour they'd been sitting there in front of an empty fireplace in the family drawing room of Stoke Bruerne House.

"I'm sorry?"

"Your thoughts, child. I can hear them from here. They have the unfortunate racket of a steam locomotive." Grandmother Bitsy wrinkled her noise. "You should really find some better thoughts before these ones give you a case of hysteria." Grandmother Bitsy flung her hand to the right as if to emphasize and pulled her knitting needle clean out of the stitches that had been made previously. She bent her head and resumed stitching even though one side no longer held any stitches.

"I wasn't thinking of anything," Eloise lied. "It's only so much change has occurred recently."

Grandmother Bitsy looked up, her eyes clear. "You're thinking Gwennie's gone off and married that sheep farmer, and now Annie's married that grim-faced duke. That leaves Ardley entirely up to you, and if you don't win his proposal, your mother will skin you alive."

Eloise swallowed. "That's putting a rather fine point on it."

But her grandmother was right. Annie had surprised all of them by marrying the Duke of Grimsby the previous week in a private ceremony by special license. The circumstances which had led up to the wedding were still rather suspicious, but Annie had seemed more herself than she had since marrying her first husband, and Eloise couldn't help but think perhaps the grim-faced duke—as her grandmother called him—might be good for Annie.

But her grandmother was correct. The pressure on Eloise to win the hand of the Duke of Ardley had just increased tenfold.

It was only her, the solitary remaining Bounds sister, who could catch the second duke on the market that season and fulfill their mother's every wish. And although Eloise was loathe to admit it, it would likely end the feud between Nancy and Viscount Bowes with Nancy coming out the winner.

Perhaps there was a book in the library which explained how one emigrated to America. Eloise should go look for it straightaway.

She didn't move, however. She remained slumped in her chair and instead reached over to the table beside her and plucked a chocolate biscuit from the plate there. She popped the entire thing into her mouth and chomped lazily.

Grandmother Bitsy pursed her lips. "Do you know when you were born I cried?"

Eloise stopped chomping. "I'm sorry?" she mumbled around the mouthful of biscuit.

"I cried," Grandmother Bitsy repeated. "I was convinced I wouldn't live long enough to see you grow up."

Slowly Eloise pushed herself up. She felt tendrils of hair come loose and fall about her shoulders as she'd had her head pressed to the back of her chair. She tucked some loose strands behind her ear and eyed her grandmother.

"That's so terribly sad. Why would you think such a thing?" Eloise asked.

Grandmother Bitsy barked a laugh. "Because I was old then and I'm older now, and I'm afraid I'm going to be disappointed again."

Eloise stared. "Disappointed? Again?"

Grandmother Bitsy gave up the pretense of knitting. "Do you recall your childhood, Eloise? I mean, with any kind of clarity?"

Eloise adjusted her shoulders and pushed another strand of loose hair behind her ear. "Of course, I do. I had a lovely childhood."

"Yes, it was terribly lovely, but do you recall what it was like growing up with your sisters?"

"Yes, I should say so." Eloise frowned in confusion, wondering if her grandmother had finally had leave of her senses.

"Gwennie was always the bold one. Do you remember? She never backed down, not even when it came to smallpox. Don't you agree?"

Eloise couldn't stop a smile as she pictured Gwen as a small child. "Even then she would fist her little hands and stick her chin out." Eloise shook her head. "I was never afraid when Gwennie was there."

Grandmother Bitsy nodded. "Exactly. And what about Annie?"

Eloise shook her head again but more emphatically this time. "Oh, Annie wasn't bold. She was...strong. When Gwennie was taken away because of the smallpox I remember being so frightened. I hid under my bed in the nursery, and Annie came and coaxed me out. She said

Gwennie would be back to boss us around in short order." Eloise smiled at the memory. "She was right."

"And what about you?"

Grandmother Bitsy's words were exact, and they had the effect of ripping Eloise from the comfort of thinking of her sisters in their childhood.

"Me?" she asked warily.

"You. Do you remember what you were like?"

Eloise shrugged. "I suppose I was like any other child. Prone to mischief with my sisters but generally obedient."

Grandmother's bark of laughter was so unexpected it sent Eloise back in her chair.

"I beg your pardon," she muttered defensively.

"You were not obedient, Eloise Cassandra." Grandmother Bitsy shook a knitting needle at her. "And that was why you were my favorite."

"I was your favorite or I am your favorite?" Eloise asked cautiously, wondering if such a question was too selfish.

Grandmother lowered her knitting needle. "I'm still not sure on that one. It depends on how you behave in the next several weeks. Your very future depends on it, and if you act foolishly, I shall be gravely disappointed and be forced to make Annie my favorite."

"You would choose a favorite amongst your grand-daughters?"

"Of course, I would."

"Heartless," Eloise whispered.

"You'll do the same when you have grandchildren. Trust me."

"I will not," Eloise declared, but her grandmother's knowing smile was disconcerting. "What does this have to do with being disappointed in me?"

"I didn't say I would be disappointed *in you*, Eloise. I said I would be disappointed." She waved the knitting needle around enough to make Eloise worry she might lose an eye. "I would never be disappointed in you. You're too predictable for such nonsense."

"Ah," Eloise scoffed incredulously, her lips parting in affront.

Now Grandmother pointed the knitting needle at her. "Go on," her grandmother challenged. "Tell me you are not feeling even more pressure now to win the hand of the Duke of Ardley."

Eloise snapped her mouth shut without saying anything.

"Precisely what I thought." Grandmother lowered her knitting needle. "Now tell me why you feel such pressure?"

Eloise held out her hands to indicate the situation. "I'm the only Bounds daughter left. Who else is going to win the gentleman's proposal?"

"Someone else entirely."

Eloise's eyes widened. "You're saying the duke won't pick me? What's wrong with me?"

Grandmother Bitsy had the nerve to roll her eyes. "There's nothing wrong with you, child. It's just you're wrong for Ardley. The man is an aristocrat in every sense of the word."

"Grandmother, I'm finding this conversation very confusing."

"You would be wasted on a man like Ardley." Again the knitting needle came out to point at Eloise accusatorially. "Your talents would go to rot in such a marriage, and I would be forced to watch you wither away."

"Grandmother," Eloise whispered, unable to say anything else.

"You, Eloise, were a wandering child, and you've grown to be an imaginative young woman. You're going to throw away that gift by marrying a stuffy duke?"

"Ardley is hardly stuffy—"

"The man is as interesting as a starched cravat."

"Grandmother." Eloise couldn't stop the whispered scold, but her grandmother seemed unfazed by it.

"You are not at all suited to the man, Eloise. You need someone with an imagination to match yours, an intellect to challenge yours, and above all a man who can set fire to your passions."

Eloise was rendered utterly mute from the grip of shock that overcame her then, but it needn't matter. Her grandmother wasn't finished.

"If you marry such a man, Eloise Cassandra, you will condemn yourself to a life of misery. Instead of a marriage, you'll be agreeing to a life in prison. You're too wild a creature for a duke, and you know it. The only question is if you will do what's right or what others wish of you."

Eloise licked her lips and pressed her hands against her thighs. Her grandmother's speech might have been passionate, but reality was a cold antidote to it.

"Grandmother, you know I wish to marry for love, but practically speaking—"

"Do you know why I married your grandfather?"

The abrupt change in subject silenced Eloise.

Grandmother Bitsy waited a moment, but as Eloise hadn't found any words, she went on. "I was with child. Did you know that? I was carrying your father when I walked down that aisle. Your grandfather and I were passionate lovers. The desire between us was scandalous. I had never felt anything so consuming in all my life, and I haven't since." She leaned forward, her gaze intense, and Eloise felt her heart hammering in her chest even as her mind blanked, unable to understand what was happening. "You might forget because I'm your grandmother, but I was young once too. I've felt desire. I've felt love. And I will tell you this now, child. If you ignore the desire and love I know you're feeling right now, you will regret it for all the rest of your life."

Eloise shook her head. "But I must marry Ardley. I'm the only one left."

Grandmother threw up both of her hands as if in resignation, but she still held her knitting needles clasped tightly and yarn went about in all directions. "Oh child, must I point out the obvious to you?" She settled her hands once more, but her eyes were a fury of consternation. "You're not the only one left, Eloise. You're not thinking of this clearly."

Eloise felt the bite of anger coursing its way through her confusion. Her grandmother had the luxury of sitting there in her old age and bestowing upon Eloise any number of platitudes, but Eloise was the one who must face reality, and the reality was she was a debutante who must secure a husband to care for her, and what better husband than a duke?

"I'm seeing things as I must, Grandmother. It's up to me to win the hand of the duke."

But Grandmother Bitsy wasn't finished. "No, child. Annie has already married the duke. Don't you see? She didn't leave you to marry Ardley. She set you free."

CHAPTER 9

Tuck stood there and wondered how much more of this he could take.

In only a short time, he would have been in London for two months.

Two. Months.

When he had first started thinking of this endeavor, he had not considered how long it might take to find a benefactor. Foolishly, he had believed London to be filled with rich gentlemen waiting for an opportunity to invest. How horribly wrong that assumption was turning out to be.

To make matters worse, he wondered if the blame lay at his feet. He wasn't so naive as to think his feelings for Eloise hadn't clouded his determination. Thoughts of her had begun to interrupt even the research he'd brought with him. Simple things like determining the number of notebooks he must pack were beyond him when he wondered absently what she might be doing just then.

To say nothing of the guilt that had surely eaten a hole directly through his stomach.

What if he'd never met Eloise?

The thought nearly made him sick. How dare he think of a life without her now? Her presence alone had opened something inside of him, and finally, for once, he had been able to release some of the worry and fear he'd never let another see.

His champagne glass was halfway to his lips when he realized what he had just thought.

Eloise.

Eloise was the one to whom he'd unburdened himself. It may have happened in a little rowboat in the middle of the Serpentine, but it had been so natural to tell her the things he'd never tell another. But then having said it, he'd wanted to tell her so much more. He wanted to tell her everything.

About how he was worried he wouldn't acclimate to the weather and be forced home or risk death.

About how he struggled with finding ways to cope with the coming darkness once the sun set for the last time that year on Spitsbergen, not to return until the following spring.

About how his greatest fear was not finding answers for Harrison.

The person he wanted beside him more than anyone on this expedition was Eloise.

He shook his head, drawing a number of curious looks, but he didn't care. Discarding his champagne glass on the tray of a passing footman, he raked his now-free hand through his hair. Eloise would not be with him in Spitsbergen. She was going to marry Liam and have lots of babies and maybe even a dog, who may or may not assault debutantes in boats.

That was what Eloise was going to do, and Tuck was going to go to the edges of the world and hope to be mauled by a polar bear rather than live life without her.

If that was a touch dramatic, he didn't care. He wanted to feel maudlin just then. He would wallow in his poor feelings as long as he wished, and then in the morning he would pick up and move on.

He adjusted his shoulders and straightened his cuffs. Enough of this foolish nonsense. He must find a benefactor.

He had almost scanned the length of the ballroom when his eyes fell on a familiar form, one which, thankfully, was wearing trousers that day.

The Earl of Renshaw stood near the periphery of the room on the other side of the wallflowers gathered around the refreshment table. While Tuck felt an instant surge of happiness at seeing the man, he was not happy to see who he was with.

The earl was penned in by none other than the Three Crusaders, students at Oxford who had given themselves such an ill-fitting title so as to rise in the esteem of their peers.

Tuck had had them in his general astronomy class the previous semester and had gotten the distinct impression they'd taken the class thinking it an easy grade. Tuck had taken great pleasure in proving them wrong.

He waited, watching carefully and assuring himself that Renshaw was a grown man and couldn't fall victim to the trio's usual pestering and tomfoolery.

But when the tallest of the young men, a Mr. Sedgewick, flicked his finger against the bottom of the earl's glass when the man tried to take a drink, sending liquid down the earl's shirtfront, Tuck moved, sliding easily through the crowd and coming to stand in front of the earl before the Three Crusaders had even finished laughing.

"Mr. Sedgewick," Tuck pronounced. "What a pleasure to see you."

The laughter died immediately when Mr. Sedgewick registered who now stood before him.

"Professor Ryan," Sedgewick said, his boisterous attitude from only moments before seemingly evaporated. "Why are you here?"

Tuck rocked back on his feet. "I believe what you meant to ask is what brings me to London. That would have been the proper address. I'm sure that's how your father would have instructed you to address one of your professors."

Mention of Sedgwick's father had been deliberate, and Tuck took no small amount of satisfaction in watching the young man's face blanche.

"Yes, exactly," Sedgewick muttered. "What brings you to London, Professor Ryan?"

"An invitation from my cousin, the Duke of Ardley." Tuck wasn't one to use Liam's name in such a way, but he would if it meant reminding young Sedgewick of his place. "I see you've met my friend, the Earl of Renshaw. Is he an acquaintance of your father's?"

Sedgewick looked away uncomfortably. Young Sedgwick's father was a baron, a destitute one, and the idea that he should be friends with an earl was a stretch.

"No, I'm afraid I only just now made the gentleman's acquaintance." Here he gave a bow to Renshaw. "And it was a pleasure meeting you, my lord. I hope our paths cross in future."

Tippy stared up at the young man, his lips slightly parted and his squint extreme as if he were watching a play and couldn't quite guess how the act was to end.

"Mr. Appleton," Tuck cut in, addressing the shorter man standing behind Sedgwick. "I trust you're working on your application of the comma. You were rather overly fond of the construction in your final term paper. I hope you're taking the summer holiday to square that away."

Mr. Appleton, a young man prone to blushing and plagued with bad teeth, only stared.

"Mr. Caruthers." Tuck moved on to the last of the Crusaders, a stocky young man whose jackets strained to remain buttoned. "I take it you've contemplated my remarks regarding your last paper, and the fact that the moon is not at the center of the universe, and that you should reserve such thinking for your creative studies."

Instead of actually responding, the man made a sound like a startled goat.

Satisfied he had made his point, Tuck smiled. "Please don't let me keep you. I'm sure there are other fascinating minds with which you three wish to engage."

Sedgwick's eyes had cleared, and he seemed to have remembered himself. "My grandfather is a great donor to the college, and he will be hearing about this."

"Oh, I hope so," Tuck said. "I'd love to speak with him about the alarming similarities between your answers on the midterm and that of your seat mate's. Shall I speak to him about that?"

Sedgwick's lips thinned, but instead of saying anything further, he nudged Appleton behind him, and together with Caruthers, wandered off into the crowd.

Tuck turned a smile on his friend. "Good evening, Tippy. I didn't expect to find you here. I thought you'd be at your club for your weekly round of whist."

Tuck had taken to visiting Tippy once a week since their introduction at the Brocklehurst garden party, and he'd come to learn a great deal about the earl. That the man favored whiskey and cream tarts and played in a whist club once a week.

Tippy patted Tuck's arm now. "I sincerely wish I were, young man, but I'm afraid tonight's hostess was a dear friend of my Carolina's. It would be remiss of me not to attend her ball."

While Tuck heard every word Tippy said, his attention was captured by the tableau over the earl's right shoulder. Just beyond the man in the corridor outside the ballroom stood Eloise. And she was gesturing at him to come with her.

Tuck shook his head and answered Tippy. "Then I'm delighted you're here."

Eloise waved more madly, sweeping her hands toward herself and then down the corridor.

"Same, same," Tippy said. "But you must excuse me. I see an old friend I must speak to before she claims a headache and disappears." Tippy waggled his eyebrows and scurried off, leaving nothing between Tuck and the madly gesturing Eloise except a few feet of empty space.

Still he shook his head.

Still she gestured for him to follow her.

He followed her.

Perhaps it was some sort of sickness. That was what compelled him to do as she bid even when he knew it to be a very bad idea.

She went left down the corridor, away from the ball, and the cacophony of the gathering slowly faded the farther they walked. When they came upon a small staircase, he thought she might make her way up it, but instead she continued straight to a door just under the stairs.

She opened the door and gestured for him to enter first. He eyed her skeptically before ducking his head inside the door, only to withdraw it.

"This is a broom cupboard."

She pointed emphatically at the cupboard. "In," she hissed.

Again, he did as she bid. He moved as far in as he could, but he didn't see how there would be room for two of them. It was a very small broom cupboard, and judging by what he could make out of it, it was built in an older part of the house with roughhewn boards gone gray with age. This he could decipher from the moonlight that came from a small square window at his back under which was a patch of fading wallpaper. He wondered if this broom cupboard had been something else once and had become the victim of a renovation. Whatever had happened, Tuck was grateful for the small patch of light as he was not inclined to frequent cupboards in the pitch black.

Eloise stepped in behind him and closed the door with a decisive snap. When she spun about to face him, moonlight fell over her eyes, and it was as though he were seeing only her soul. He felt himself pitching forward even as he didn't move, but then she spoke.

"We mustn't see each other anymore."

He blinked. "You were the one who lured me into this broom cupboard."

He knew that wasn't what she meant, but her words had cut something inside of him, and he thought sarcasm might keep the pieces together a little longer.

She closed her eyes briefly before opening them again. "You know what I mean. My sister, Annie, married Grimsby, Tuck. That leaves only me to marry…to marry…" She licked her lips, her eyes moving away from his face, and he could almost feel her dread, predict her next words. "To marry your cousin."

He knew her word choice to be deliberate, and he could only respect her for it. Because she was right. Liam was courting Eloise, and Tuck was…what was Tuck doing?

Stealing pieces of her to which he had no right? Trading stolen moments for a lifetime that wasn't his?

"You're right." The words were easier to say when he

reminded himself of his betrayal. "I had heard about your sister, and you are right. We cannot do this."

He thought her eyes might have widened, but the moonlight was tricky in a broom cupboard.

"Yes, I am," she said. "No more helping each other. No more agreements. Nothing. We cannot be seen together anymore. We've already put ourselves in too much danger, and we're lucky we were never caught."

Danger? Is that how she thought of it?

Because that had never once entered his mind. When he thought of their stolen moments, he could only think of wonder and magic and worst of all, love. Never danger.

But she was right. If they had been caught, she would be forced to marry him, and he would ruin her life. He had no funds beyond his meager allowance. He was a professor of all things. That was no life for someone like Eloise.

"I agree." How the words didn't shred his throat he'd never know. "Eloise, I—" But it seemed those were all the words he had because he couldn't look at her in the moonlight anymore. This beautiful woman who had so mysteriously entered his life when it was already too late.

"I hope you have a wonderful life with Liam. I truly do." His words hung between them, and something happened to her eyes, a light sparking in them only to die quickly to a mere ember.

He thought she would say something, but instead she shook her head, and he thought he saw tears in her eyes now, but she spun around too quickly for him to see, and then she was reaching for the door, turning the knob, and this magical interlude in his dull life would be over.

But the knob didn't turn.

He watched her, her hand struggling, the other going up to push against the door.

Nothing.

"Tuck." The sound of his name, harsh and low, was like yelling fire in a crowded ball. She shoved against the door, turned the knob. Nothing.

"Move." He squeezed beside her, braced himself against the door, and tried the knob, but he knew almost at once it was of no use. "Eloise, I'm afraid to tell you this."

She shoved at his shoulder. "Try again. You must try again." She was trying to get around him, her arms pushing around him even though there was no space to move.

He seized her arms, drawing them down her sides and pulling her into his embrace if only to stop her from hurting herself.

"Eloise, listen to me," he said, and then when her eyes finally lifted to his, he said the thing that would end everything. "We're locked in."

* * *

Locked in.

The words reverberated in her mind like the ringing of a bell, the same pitch and cadence played over and over again.

"No." She pushed Tuck's hands aside to grip the doorknob once more, but again, it wouldn't twist beneath her hand. She wedged her shoulder between the door and the jamb to gain better leverage, using both hands this time to turn the knob.

Nothing.

Locked in.

It wasn't supposed to happen like this. She had come here tonight with such resolve, so cool of emotion. In fact, there was to be no emotion at all. Emotion was too dangerous when it came to Tuck. There could be none of it when she ended whatever it was that was happening between them.

Love.

She knew it for what it was but had been too scared to speak it.

But now...

Locked in.

She spun around, or at least, tried to. The cramped space afforded little when it came to demonstrative emotional outbursts.

"We can't be locked in. We can't. You must get this door open. We can't be found like this. We'll—"

But she couldn't finish the sentence. There was the smallest window behind Tuck, and moonlight fell through it, casting enough of a glow for her to see his face. There was a pain there, an unfathomable one, and she knew if she finished her sentence it would be the greatest unkindness to someone who didn't deserve such cruelty.

Because the worst of it would be that it wasn't true.

Forced to wed.

How tragic to even think it. To marry Tucker Ryan would be her greatest dream, and she could never make him believe otherwise.

So she didn't say it. She simply stood there, staring at him in the moonlight just as she'd done the first time they'd met, but this time with a great deal less apprehension.

She set you free.

Her grandmother's words came back to her then, and she felt them as she hadn't that day in the drawing room. Her grandmother was right even if Eloise hadn't wanted to see it then. Annie had released Eloise by marrying a duke. That would need to be enough now.

She didn't realize she was crying until he reached up and with his thumb brushed the tears from her cheeks. She couldn't stop herself. She leaned into him, her cheek finding the place where it fit so perfectly into his palm, and for one second she believed everything wasn't falling apart around them.

"Annie's married, Tuck. I'm the only one left to win Ardley's proposal. It's all up to me, and I can't be a silly girl who believes in love anymore. I must face the future and what's expected of me. There's no one else left." The last of her words caught on a sob, and she gave in, burying her head against his chest.

His arms came around her, one going into her hair to hold her against him, the other around her waist to pull her close.

He whispered things to her she couldn't understand through the sound of her own tears, but it didn't matter. She was in precisely the right place when the world fell apart.

She had been so certain in seeking out Tuck that night. Ending things was the only rational action to take. She couldn't do it anymore. She couldn't help him, not after everything that had happened.

Now it was over.

For they would be discovered. Dear heavens, she *hoped* they were discovered. How long must they wait in a broom cupboard?

Slowly she became aware of what Tuck was actually saying, and his words had her drawing back.

She blinked at him. "You were really planning to live in the Arctic so you wouldn't be forced to see me and Ardley married?"

The haunted look that had so recently filled his gaze was gone, replaced with a sad kind of resignation. Why hadn't she thought of that? Her goal that entire season was to marry this man's *cousin*. Why had she never once thought of what that would mean?

She knew now how close the two of them were, and if Eloise were married to Ardley, she would be forced to be around Tuck a great deal. Why hadn't she even considered it? It would be *torture* to see this man while married to another.

"Oh Tuck." The words were hardly whispered, and yet her voice was still heavy with tears, but she couldn't think of anything else to say. So she didn't. For once, she let Tuck speak.

He cupped her face in both hands now, and she forced herself to listen and stop her silly crying.

"I promise you I will find a way to provide for you. I have an allowance from my father, and Oxford affords—"

She gripped his wrists. "You mustn't worry about that. I'm not. At the very worst, my father would be happy to provide a place for us in his home—" She stopped, the words jamming against the back of her teeth as she realized what she was saying. "Oh no, I can't possibly live with my mother." She shook her head even though Tuck's hands remained where they were, cupping her cheeks. "I can't live with my mother. She's a lovely woman, but you've met her. Her personality would overflow a barge, and really it's quite a lot."

His lips turned up just the slightest bit at this, and suddenly it didn't seem quite like the entire world was ending. Just the one she had imagined.

"I've ruined your life." She spoke when she realized she hadn't intended to, but with those words something lifted from her chest like an admission of guilt.

He shifted his hands, pressed his thumbs to her lips. "Don't say that. My life would have been ruined without you in it."

She shook her head, and he let his hands slip away. "How can you say that? Before this season, you didn't even know I existed."

He studied her, and she wondered how much he could see in so little light. But then his eyes were shifting back and forth as though he were reading something she couldn't see. "I think somehow I knew you were out there. And if I didn't know, my body knew because it recognized you the moment you sprang out of that hedge in the courtyard and nearly gave me a heart attack."

Impossibly she felt a smile pulling at her lips. "Gave you a heart attack? I thought you were a ghoul from one of Dante's seven circles of Hell."

His face turned boyish then, and she remembered that night in the courtyard, so long ago now, when she had thought him playful.

"A ghoul? Why would you think that?"

"You had red eyes."

His expression fell, his countenance turning serious. "I suppose that is true. Excellent observation, Lady Eloise." His brow furrowed. "And what did you expect me to do, being a ghoul as it were?"

"Steal my soul." She said it plainly, not feeling at all foolish to tell him the truth.

"What if I steal your heart instead?"

His words traveled straight to the part of her that warmed at the mere sight of him.

"Tucker Ryan, you're being romantic again."

"And so what if I am?" He nodded in the direction of the door. "When someone comes to let us out, there will be scandal that can only be stopped by our marriage. You know that. Would it be so terrible if it were a happy one?"

"How can it?" She licked her lips, suddenly feeling the enormity of what was about to happen clogged in her throat. "We've done a horrible thing. We've betrayed the trust of people who matter to us."

He gripped her shoulders now and squeezed reassuringly. "It's not anything that hasn't happened before, and it's not as though we didn't try to stop it." He shook his head, slowly, almost in astonishment. "I just don't think love can be stopped, Eloise."

Everything inside of her stilled as her eyes rounded. "You love me?" It was little more than a whisper, and she hated how her confidence fled in that moment, but there was something about gazing upon this man in the moonlight that did things to her.

"I do love you, Eloise Bounds. I hope that's enough for you."

She waited a beat, thinking this all a horrible trick the universe hoped to play on her. That the most wonderful thing to ever happen to her couldn't possibly be true, and any second he would disappear, having never been there in her arms at all. But he didn't disappear, and he didn't take back the words that had found their way to her heart.

"Say it again."

A grin tipped up one side of his mouth while his eyes seemed to absorb her, and she realized she should have told him she loved him back.

She gripped the lapels of his jacket. "I've wanted this my whole life, and I just want to hear you say it again."

"But how can you? You didn't know me before this season."

"Tucker Ryan, do not make me beg."

"Matthew. My middle name is Matthew. If you're going to scold me, do it properly."

Now it was her turn to grin. "Tucker Matthew Ryan, tell me you love me."

He leaned down, and she thought he might kiss her, but instead he whispered against her lips, "You first."

She laughed, and somehow her arms wound themselves around his neck as she hung on to him. "I love you," she said. And then, "I love you, Tucker Matthew Ryan."

"I love you, Eloise—" He leaned back just enough.

"Cassandra," she supplied.

"Really?" He tilted his head to one side. "I wouldn't have thought it." He leaned back even farther. "Do you wish to secure the gift of sight from me? For I promise you, I do not have it to give."

She smiled now, truly, wondering if this would be how it always was between them. This back and forth that came so easily, nothing ever moving in a straight line, going wherever their whimsy carried them.

"I shouldn't want it even if you had it on offer. I find I like the surprise of you."

His smile warmed then, and he bent his head back down. She readied herself for his kiss, but it never came. Because just then the door rattled, sending her nearly into the ceiling in fright.

She turned and faced it as though she were facing her executioner, but Tuck still held one of her hands, and she curled her fingers into his.

With a great jarring splinter of wood, the door came free with a mild curse and puff of air.

Lady Travers, the woman whose house they stood in, was expected. She held an old iron key in one hand, examining it as though she hadn't anticipated it would work any longer. She turned her gaze slowly on the broom cupboard. There was nowhere for Tuck and Eloise to hide even if they should wish it, so Eloise kept hold of Tuck's hand and stepped into the light.

"Lady Travers, I believe I got locked in your broom cupboard. You must see to it should any of your other guests fall victim to the same circumstance." Where such bravado came from, Eloise couldn't have said, but Grandmother Bitsy was always telling her people were often confused by a display of confidence. Perhaps some part of Eloise believed they could still come out of this unscathed.

But at the sound of the second voice, the one coming from just beyond the door, so that Eloise hadn't seen her standing there, what little bit of hope she had left vanished.

"Is that so?" Rosemary Hayes-Martin, Viscountess Bowes said.

Eloise looked her directly in the eye and raising her chin, she said, "Viscountess Bowes, I didn't see you there. Will you allow me to introduce you to my betrothed?"

CHAPTER 10

Three days later, in the muted light of their rented rooms, the romantic words they had exchanged that night in the broom cupboard had lost their luster.

"It's…modest," Eloise said as she bent to sit on the edge of their bed.

The mattress dipped, sending Eloise sprawling backward. Tuck lurched forward to pull her back up, but the lovely hat she had worn to their wedding ceremony that morning toppled off the side of the bed and disappeared somewhere between the sagging bed and the wardrobe with the broken door that was pushed into the corner.

He held both of her hands as he helped her to sit more securely on the edge of the worn-out mattress. When she finally met his gaze, he expected to see regret there, but then she laughed, the sound light and wholly unfitted to the sad little room.

Liam had offered them residence at his home, but Tuck's pride wouldn't allow him to take his bride back there after they were wed, and so he'd found the only rooms his meager funds could afford. They were in Bloomsbury and on just the

141

right side of shabby, but he had paid for the lease himself, and at least for a month, there would be a roof over his wife's head.

His wife.

He returned her gaze as her laugh faded around them and took a seat next to her on the mattress, pitching his legs to keep from rolling into her.

"Modest is rather a generous word for it." He looked about the small space that was directly off the kitchen and parlor before looking back at his wife. "I don't suppose you know how to cook?"

"I haven't the slightest idea," she said, another laugh escaping her lips. She pressed a hand to her forehead. "Oh Tuck, what have we done?"

They had been wed by special license, of course. Liam had called in any number of favors to see the license procured, and a dozen more to find a clergyman in time to see the deed through. Lady Stoke Bruerne would have had it happen immediately if only to quell any gossip with the swiftness of the marriage.

Their sudden betrothal had not garnered the animosity Tuck had expected, but then, he wasn't sure there had been time for it. Eloise had been right that night in the broom cupboard. Her mother, although perfectly pleasant, could be rather formidable when the situation called for it.

It had been much the same with Liam. Tuck shuddered to think of the debt he owed his cousin, the one required from Tuck's betrayal. He wasn't sure what he had expected from his cousin when Tuck revealed the truth to him, but it wasn't what he had gotten.

Liam had been nothing but congratulatory and then left at once to get the license.

It had all happened so fast and so unexpectedly. Tuck wasn't even sure how they had come to be in this strange place, these little rooms in Bloomsbury. But they had agreed to save Eloise's dowry. As Tuck's allowance and earnings from his position at Oxford were so modest, they had felt it best to have some sort of cushion they could rely on in hard times.

But as they sat there, blinking into what little afternoon light made its way between the buildings and through the narrow windows of the room, he wasn't sure if this wasn't hard times they found themselves in.

He took Eloise's hand. "I'm not sure it's something we've done or something that would have happened eventually with or without our doing." He tried to smile, but it felt forced and too close to lying so he stopped.

She squeezed his hand though. "You might be right, I think. Did you get a chance to speak to Ardley? Was he terribly upset?"

"I'm afraid there wasn't time. What wasn't taken up by securing the special license was arguing with him about taking up residence in his home after our wedding."

It still felt strange to say that. *Our wedding.* He couldn't possibly mean his own. Only other people were meant to be married.

But somehow he was sitting there, next to his wife, and his wife was Eloise. He couldn't quite believe it and wondered if it would ever seem real or if he would always marvel at the idea of it.

"It was much the same with my mother, I'm afraid. She was overwrought at the idea that there would be no time to plan a grand wedding. I never got the chance to speak to her about it really. It was all very..."

"Mechanical," he supplied, feeling the weight of the word press down on his shoulders.

Eloise laughed, and again, it sounded bizarre in that strange place, but this time not quite as bizarre. The sound seemed to chisel at the melancholy that hung about him, and he smiled, genuinely this time.

She nudged his shoulder with her own. "This will be quite the romantic story we tell our grandchildren." She held her hands up, indicating the space about them. "It was a whirl-wind wedding, and afterward, your grandfather swept me away to a place I'd never been before." She turned to look at him, and the light in her eyes dispelled the rest of his melancholy. "I suppose we should leave out some of the details, don't you think?"

He laughed now even when he thought he would never laugh again. He touched his wife's face, tracing the curve of her cheek.

"I hardly think they should know *all* of the details. It would be nice to retain at least a little mystery." He was still smiling when he kissed her, and he was surprised to find the lingering guilt that had plagued him since discovering her true identity was no longer there.

She was just Eloise, his wife, and the press of betrayal was a little further away now.

"Well," Eloise said when he leaned back, and she pushed to her feet, hands on her knees. "I suppose we must be practical about this."

She strode over to what was supposed to be the kitchen, which while it was located through a small archway, there wasn't any true separation of that space from the bedroom area, so he reclined on the bed and watched her, wondering what she might do.

She proceeded to the small cast iron stove and gingerly plucked at one of the plates only to send it clattering back to the stove top when her finger came away smudged with soot.

She turned to him, her nose wrinkled. "We use this for cooking, don't we?" She eyed the plate that had so recently soiled her finger. "I should think we haven't much choice in the matter, do we?"

Although he found the spectacle amusing, he decided to give her a break.

"There's enough in our funds to procure our food from the tearoom across the street. I don't think between the two of us it will be enough of an expense to send us straight into poverty."

Her eyebrows climbed nearly to her hairline. "I should hope not. I doubt I would make it in the poor house." She peered down at herself. "I'm really not cut out for it."

He gained his feet and went to her, picking up her hands and squeezing them. "Eloise Bounds, I think you're a great deal stronger than you let on."

"Eloise Ryan, thank you very much," she corrected him with a smile. "And do you truly believe that?"

He shrugged. "Well, I must think that. Otherwise come autumn, I must leave you behind, and I like that idea a great deal less."

She blinked. "Leave me behind?"

"When I go to Spitsbergen. It isn't a place for a lady."

She tugged her hands free. "Tucker Ryan, do not even think it. I will not be left here to rot in London while you go off adventuring. I'm coming with you."

"It's cold there."

She raised her chin. "I thrive in cold weather."

"Food will be rationed, and then it will be a great deal of fish and dried and salted meats."

One eyebrow went up. "Debutantes are trained on starvation tactics."

"There are polar bears."

She shook her head. "You've met my mother. A polar bear should be no trouble."

He gazed at her, trying to picture her in the Arctic. "I

don't know what drew us together that night in the court-yard, but I can't help but feel it was meant to be."

She stood on tiptoe then and wrapped her arms around his neck, pressing her body against him. "I think it was too." She shook her head again. "I've never gone out into the courtyard at night like that. I just suddenly felt like I needed fresh air, or I would expire." She combed her fingers through his hair, and he felt it flop back on his forehead. "I found a great deal more than fresh air, however."

He bent his head and skimmed her lips with his, not quite kissing her. "And are you disappointed in what you found?"

She smiled, and he could feel her eyes flutter shut before she shifted, capturing his lips even as he tried to teasingly pull away. She laughed and wound her arms more tightly about him, deepening the kiss.

He stumbled backward, pulling her with him until they fell upon the bed. He rolled her beneath him, savoring the way her leg slipped so easily between his, coiling her body around him. Her arms went from around his neck to slip beneath his jacket, her fingers curling into his waistcoat as she pulled him atop her.

The kiss went on and on, and he could sense they were both reluctant to end it, but Eloise was right. They must be practical, and after the long day they'd had, they must seek sustenance.

He was forced to wrench his mouth free and even then, he placed a wandering hand along the line of her bodice to keep her from chasing after him.

"We must stop. I must feed my wife before she expires. I don't care what starvation tactics you learned as a debutante. You must eat."

Even in the muted light, her face glowed with happiness, and he was not too modest to admit a great deal of arousal. But he hadn't a clue when the tearoom closed for the day, and it would be best if they were to figure out their new living situation.

He sat up, ready to push them from the bed when something else happened entirely.

She moved so quickly he had no time to prepare. One minute she was flat on her back, and the next she had toppled him over and straddled him. She perched there above him, a self-satisfied smirk on her face.

"I am hungry, Mr. Ryan," she said in a voice he'd never heard from her before, a voice that dripped with sensuality. She placed her hand against his chest just above his waistcoat, and then with two fingers marched a line up to his cravat. With the same fluidity she had shown in besting him, she whipped the cravat from around his neck before bracing her hand still holding the cravat against the bed just beside his head, bringing her so close he could feel her breath against his ear as she whispered, "But it's not for food," as her fingers went to work on the buttons of his shirt.

* * *

Two months.

That was how long she'd been denied this.

No, more than that. She'd made herself believe she didn't *want* this.

That had been a lie, and the worst kind. The kind one tells oneself.

But she needn't lie anymore. She needn't deny herself.

Tuck was hers, all of him and time willing, forever.

The shabbiness of their rented rooms was quickly forgotten. The pain she'd felt for three whole days since their treachery had been discovered was somehow gone, vanished beneath the touch of her husband.

Her husband.

What a beautiful thing that was.

For a second, she felt selfish. All the people they had hurt to get to this point and yet all she could feel just then was pure and simple bliss. But perhaps that was all right. Perhaps it was good even for her to make the best of what had happened. She loved Tuck, and he loved her, and it wasn't as though they had set out to hurt the people they loved.

It had just…happened.

After everything, after all they had pent up and ignored, she had expected this moment to be, well, more than it was turning out to be. She had expected explosions and fireworks, but it wasn't that. Had she been thinking about her husband and who he truly was, she would have known better. Because instead of fireworks, he did something far more.

He *savored* her.

While she tried to remove his waistcoat and shirt, he'd stopped her, catching her hands with one of his as he rolled them. Now he perched atop her, a solitary finger tracing the curve of her cheek as he studied her.

"Do you know what the first thing about you was that I loved?" he whispered.

She shook her head, unable to form words.

His finger rose over the crest of her nose. "Your freckles," he said, his finger falling to the other side and tracing a path through those very freckles. "You looked as though you had swallowed the universe, and the stars shown through your skin right here." He tapped her cheek as his eyes lifted to hers. "And I thought only someone as spectacular as you could contain the fathoms of the universe."

"You're being romantic again," she accused, her voice tight with the fire he stoked in her at a single touch.

His smile was slow to come as he continued to study her.

"That keeps happening around you. Perhaps it's not my fault but yours."

She laughed, the sound so precious as it cut through the strange noises around them, the ones that came with their home that she wasn't quite used to. But laughter, it held the power to make anything familiar.

They undressed each other then, taking turns by some unspoken agreement. It was as though they were discovering each other, one piece of clothing at a time, and it should have been difficult, awkward, and uncomfortable. But it was none of those things. With each piece he removed from her, she felt more like herself, braver and free, until she gave all of herself to him.

That wasn't to say she didn't take because she did. Of course, she did.

In all of their stolen touches, she'd never felt his bare skin, not in this way, and it was like touching flame, and there was no saving herself from the burn of it. She freed him of his waistcoat and shirt first, greedy to feel the muscles of his chest under her fingertips, to explore the planes of his back and shoulders until she knew him better than her own body.

But touching him wasn't enough. She needed to taste him.

She pressed her lips to his neck as he worked to free her from her corset, and the heat there was shocking, sending electricity clear through her from a single taste. She kept going, along this shoulder, down his chest, tasting the salt of him.

But once her corset was off, he robbed her of her exploration as he undertook his own, pushing each strap of her chemise from her shoulders until the garment fell, clinging to her breasts. She watched his face then, watched his eyes smolder as he studied her, and let the sheer sensuality of the moment overtake her.

"Tuck," she whispered, daring to touch his face, wanting him to look into her eyes with such passion.

But when he looked up, the passion was gone. It was replaced with something far greater.

Love.

And it traveled directly to her heart, wrapping her in the beauty of it.

"Oh Tuck," she whispered again, and he kissed her.

There was the passion. It was in his kiss, in his touch as his fingers played with her fallen chemise, as he helped lower it while somehow keeping his fingers from touching her.

She moaned against his mouth, arched into him, and still he escaped her. It wasn't until the chemise lay pooled at her hips that he finally broke the kiss and sat up. She hadn't known how much pleasure there would be in watching him watch her, but it was there, stoking the fire inside of her, and she thought she could get lost in the way he looked at her. Looked at her with love and respect and fascination.

Fascination.

No one had ever looked at her like that.

Maybe only Tuck could see her that way because this thing between them had been meant to be all along. For a moment she wondered if they had been wrong to fight it. If they should have admitted their feelings before it had taken the course it had.

She pushed the thoughts away. Now wasn't the time to think of such things. This was the reality of their situation, and it was fruitless to think on what ifs.

Besides, her husband had lifted her hips and was working her chemise off of her. She watched him, the way he pursued his goal so intently, a true academic at work. And then when it slipped over her feet, the way he flung it carelessly aside.

She giggled, unable to help herself, and he looked at her, a wicked gleam in his eye.

She expected him to pounce on her now that he'd stripped her bare, but he didn't. Instead he leaned over her, looming above her, and she wondered at just how broad of shoulder he was, blocking out what little light made it through the shabby curtains at the window.

"Mrs. Ryan, do you find me amusing?"

She tried to loop her arms about his neck, pull him close, but he dodged out of her grasp, sitting up enough so she was forced to trail her fingers through the smattering of hair on his chest. His eyes fluttered shut briefly, so she figured it wasn't so terrible a tradeoff.

"I find much about you amusing, Mr. Ryan, but right now I'm thinking other things about you."

His eyes opened, and he met her gaze unflinchingly. "And just what are those things?"

"I think—"

He touched her, just a finger at the edge of her collarbone. He let it dip, sweeping down her chest.

"I think—" she tried again, but then that finger moved between her breasts, barely touching her, skimming her skin so she was forced to chase after it, but that only made him pull his hand back to keep the balance, touching her just enough but not enough at the same time.

She wanted him to cup her breasts, to stroke her nipples. Her body ached for his attention, but he deliberately denied her, his finger moving lazily down her torso, dipping into her belly button, and lower still. Her legs fell away for him, bidding him to touch her, but he didn't.

Instead, he came above her, blocking out the remaining light as he imprisoned her between his arms, one hand on either side of her head.

"What were you trying to say, Mrs. Ryan?" he whispered, his mouth playing with the lobe of one ear.

"I didn't say anything." Was that her whimpering?

"But you meant to say something." He sucked the lobe of her ear into her mouth, and she came up off the bed, her arms going around his waist, her fingers digging into his back.

"I…I…" But whatever she had been trying to say dissolved into a moan, and perhaps that was what she had meant all along.

Because his lips moved lower, down her neck, over her chest, and—

"Oh God!" The cry sprang from her lips as he sucked first one nipple into his mouth and then the other. Her hands scrambled against his back, trying to pull herself closer to him, as if she could give him any more of herself.

The tension coiling in her tightened, and her legs moved of their own volition, wrapping around him, lifting her to him.

He chuckled against the underside of her breast where he plied hot, wet kisses. "That's another thing I love about you, Mrs. Ryan." He swept up her body so quickly, the breath caught in her throat. "Your eagerness," he growled and captured her mouth with his.

That was when he touched her.

He touched her right in the place that ached most for him. She didn't know how he knew, but her body seemed to pulse for him, and he'd placed his finger directly atop it.

"Tuck." She ripped her lips from his, sucking in a breath. "Tuck, I—"

His finger moved, circling her nub, and the pleasure bordered on pain. But he didn't let up. His finger circled and rubbed, and her hips moved, pushing herself against him.

"Tuck, I—" It wasn't enough, but it was all too much at the same time.

When he entered her, she thought it would hurt. That somehow he wouldn't fit properly. But her body knew things she did not, and with him came a pleasing pressure that swept through in a warm wave. She exhaled, pleasure leaving her body in a hush as it readied itself for more.

"Eloise." His lips were pressed to her neck, and she felt the muscles of his back go rigid the moment he'd pushed into her.

He kept circling her nub as he withdrew and pushed into her again, slowly, achingly slowly, and then again. The tension she thought couldn't get any more tightly wound pressed in on itself to a single point, and she knew something must happen or else...or else...

"Tuck, I need..." But she didn't know what it was she needed.

He moved faster, sliding in and out of her as his hand worked her most sensitive place. The tension changed, crescendoed, until—

When she fell apart, it was with a perfectness she could have only found with Tuck. It was with a rightness that had been there from the beginning, and it was no surprise that it would happen now, like this, when they were together in the basest way possible.

Tears leaked from the corners of her eyes, and she turned her head, hoping to hide them in the pillow, but he caught her, his hands cupping her face as he rested on his elbows.

"Eloise, I hurt you," he whispered.

She shook her head furiously. "No, no, it isn't that. It was just—" She faced him then. "I waited so long for this, and I don't know why it hurts so much. This love I have for you."

Relief came into his face as he must have realized he hadn't hurt her, and he smiled. "It hurts because big feelings need space. You're just learning how to carry your love. That's all." He kissed her softly. "Just give it time."

She tried to smile back at him, but the ache of her love

was so great. It was a moment before she realized he had stopped.

"Are we…finished?" she asked, feeling suddenly shy for the first time in her life.

"Not exactly," he said, a sheepish grin on his face.

It was then she understood he was still hard inside of her, and heat crept up her cheeks.

"Do you mean…you can do that again? I mean, what you did to me. That can happen…again?"

His smile was wicked now. "Of course, it can."

And it did happen.

And it happened again and again and again until darkness flooded their little rooms, and they fell asleep in each other's arms, exhausted.

CHAPTER 11

When a knock sounded on the door of their rooms, Eloise did the sensible thing and held the hand towel she'd been folding up like a shield in front of her and stared at the door as if she'd never seen one before in her life.

Tuck had left early that morning to attend a lecture at City College, after which he was to attend a meeting of the Royal Astronomical Society. He had invited her along, but she wanted to take the opportunity to make a home of sorts of their rooms while he was out. It was incredible what she *didn't* know about homemaking. Perhaps she could ask Annie for help in finding some books on the topic.

But all of this was to say Eloise was alone when the knock came at the door, and she felt suddenly exposed like she hadn't since her wedding day the previous week. It was a strange thing, leaving one's family and the only home one had known since their birth and shifting one's entire life to a new place and a new kind of family.

The caller was forced to knock again while Eloise sorted

her thoughts, and it was as though the second knock pulled her from them.

She strode to the door and only at the last moment recalled her wits and the need for caution as she was, indeed, alone. "Who is it?" she asked.

"It's Gwennie, Eloise."

Again Eloise stared at the door. A handful of seconds ticked by before she could remember how to unlock the thing and open it, and then—

"Gwennie," Eloise whispered, her shock a tangible thing as it spread through her body.

Standing there on her doorstep was the one person she had wished to speak to the most through this whole tumultuous thing, and for a moment Eloise couldn't believe it was real. But it was. Gwen was there.

Eloise stepped forward and threw her arms around her sister, forgetting she should have invited her in and closed the door for privacy's sake. But Eloise didn't care a wit about privacy just then. She wanted to hug her sister.

Gwen's arms were strong when they closed around her, and—

Eloise pulled back ever so slightly. "Do you smell of hay?"

Gwen's smile was quick. "Esmeralda decided to deliver just as I was about to leave, and I couldn't leave the poor creature in a state like that." Gwen extracted herself and waved at the door for Eloise to retreat back into their rooms. Gwen followed, still talking. "And after the debacle with Sugar Cane and Blue Belle last week, I couldn't think of leaving Logan in such a state, so I popped over the fence and helped Hatrick with the delivery." Gwen strode across the small space that was the kitchen, plucking her gloves from her hands one finger at a time, her eyes scanning the room quickly before turning about. "I was already in my traveling gown though, as you can imagine, and—" She shrugged. "Here we are."

Father had married Gwen off to a sheep farmer at the beginning of the season, Logan Bender, the Earl of Gracey, and it was rather a pleasant surprise that the union turned out to be a love match. The pair had come to London for their introduction ball, and although Eloise had been preoccupied with her predicament of falling in love with the wrong man she hadn't missed how much Gwen and Logan loved each other. She was happy for her sister. Even if she smelled of hay.

Gwen flicked her gloves around to indicate the room. "Is this really where you're living?" Gwen turned a full circle, again taking in the space, and for one split second, Eloise felt shame creep up her neck. Gwen was a countess now after all, and she might have changed her standards since marrying Gracey. But then her sister turned back around, her smile brilliant. "How exciting." She tossed aside the gloves as she took one of the two chairs at the scarred wooden table pushed into the corner. "Tell me. Are you really going with him to Spitsbergen?"

She laid her gloves and hat on the table and looked up expectantly, and Eloise wondered how she could ever doubt her sister's loyalty even for a second.

Eloise slipped into the chair opposite Gwen. "I shall as long as he secures the funding he needs before the autumn."

"Oh, I wish I had made it for the wedding, but Mother's letter said it happened quickly."

Eloise let the heat infuse her cheeks. "Yes, I'm afraid it did. Last week, in fact." When Eloise met her sister's gaze again, it was to see mirth in her eyes. "Gwennie, really," Eloise scolded.

But Gwen only laughed. "Oh Eloise, you must admit it's rather exciting. You were always the most dutiful one. The joy I got when I received Mother's letter saying you were being married by special license to avoid scandal." Gwen leaned across the table conspiratorially. "Just how much scandal was there to avoid?"

Eloise swallowed. "Enough to have Mother taking a vow of silence should she ever find out about it."

Gwen's laugh then was contagious, and Eloise felt lighter than she had in days.

She snatched her sister's hand from where it lay on the table. "Oh Gwennie, I'm so glad you've come." Eloise paused, concern creeping into her joy. "Why are you here?"

Gwen's smile faded. "It's about Mother."

Eloise let go of her sister's hand and shrank back in her seat. "I've disappointed her."

Gwen straightened and dropped her hands to her lap. "Well, that's what I've come to talk to you about. I'm well aware of Mother's intentions for you and Annie this season, and I can see how you might think Mother would be disappointed in your choice." Gwen paused as if considering. "Especially given that your husband is the cousin of the gentleman Mother wished you to marry."

"You can see how things were rather tricky this season," Eloise muttered.

"Tricky indeed," Gwen said, a little of the previous mirth coming to her lips. "I had wondered why you seemed to be absent even in your letters. Scandal explains a great deal."

Eloise could only look at her hands as she picked at one of the scars on the tabletop. "I know, Gwennie. I promise I'll apologize to Mother. There simply wasn't time before the wedding and since then..." She gathered her courage and looked up. "Well, I haven't exactly figured out how to do it. I've dashed all her dreams. If I had married Ardley, Mother would have had the coup of the season. Can you imagine how she would have lorded that over Viscountess Bowes?"

Gwen's expression had grown more concerned through Eloise's explanation, and Eloise couldn't help but feel she'd been right about her mother's disappointment.

"So that's why you've come?" Eloise asked now. "To see that I make reparations for my behavior?"

Gwen appeared suddenly repulsed as though she'd unexpectedly inhaled the aroma of sheep dung. "Oh heavens, no. You didn't drown a litter of puppies, Eloise. You only fell in love."

"With the wrong man." Eloise hissed the words as if saying them aloud would condemn her again.

"And who is to say who is the wrong man and the right one? I find myself married to a man I didn't even know existed a short time ago, and I'm absolutely besotted with the idiot. How would one characterize such an occurrence?"

Eloise only blinked. She thought her sister to be in love, but besotted was another thing entirely.

Gwen reached out and stopped Eloise from splintering the table into pieces with her bare hands. "But that's not why I've come. While you were preoccupied with your scandal, I learned something from Mother that I think you should know."

"What is it?" For the first time since she'd heard the knock at the door, Eloise feared this might not be about her.

"Our mother wished for me to have a season," Gwen stated plainly.

Eloise blinked. Again. "I'm sorry?"

"A season," Gwen repeated. "Did you know as much? She wished for me to debut."

Gwen was firmly on the shelf before marrying, having never had a season, when Father announced he'd arranged a marriage for her. Eloise had always assumed neither of her parents wished to put the eldest Bounds daughter through the torture cruel debutantes could inflict on one another during the social requirements of a season. Gwen was too much of a target with her smallpox scars.

"But I thought Mother and Father wished to protect you," Eloise said.

"Father apparently did, but Mother wanted me to debut. According to Grandmother Bitsy, it's the only thing Mother has ever relented on."

"Huh," Eloise muttered, thinking it over. "Why do you think Mother wished for you to debut?"

"According to Father, it was only after he promised Mother he'd find me a match a different way that Mother gave in."

"I don't understand," Eloise said.

Gwen squeezed her hand then. "Can't you see? It's not that Mother wished for us to make good matches that would elevate our titles. She simply wanted us to be matched."

Eloise wrinkled her brow. "I'm still confused."

"If Father hadn't promised to find me a husband, Mother never would have given in. She wanted to ensure I would have someone to share this life with, whoever that may be. The title didn't matter to her. Not really. It was only that her daughters shouldn't be alone."

Eloise couldn't believe her. She simply couldn't. "But Mother wanted us to marry the dukes. To triumph over Viscountess Bowes."

Gwen smiled. "Of course, she would want that. But do you really think she'd be upset that you *fell in love*?"

"How do you know it's love?" Eloise whispered, somehow afraid she'd been caught stealing hair ribbons from her mother's dressing table.

Gwen laughed. "We all know it's love, little sister. It's rather obvious. You were found in a broom cupboard with him."

"Does Mother know it's love?" Somehow this idea was worse than disappointing her mother in the first place.

"I would wager she does." Gwen squeezed her hand once more. "It will make it easier for you to talk to her now, don't you think? Now that you understand she already knows you fell in love?"

Eloise shook her head. "You're making a lot of assumptions, Gwennie."

"They're not assumptions when they're based on facts." She squeezed Eloise's hand one more time before getting to her feet. "I asked Mother to arrange a dinner while I'm in town. You and Tuck will come, yes?"

It was a moment before Eloise realized her sister had asked a question. "Yes, yes, of course," she said, not really understanding what she was agreeing to.

"Good." Gwen gathered her hat and gloves. "I'd like to see my sisters and these new husbands they've acquired while I've been off in Yorkshire."

Gwen was halfway to the door before Eloise remembered to stand and show her sister out.

Eloise opened the door, but Gwen stalled, turning back to her.

"Tell Mother you love him, Eloise. She'll understand." Her sister paused, concern writ across her brow. "Eloise, you're happy, aren't you? With what's happened?"

Eloise looked at her sister then, and it was as though she'd been pulled directly from the fog of her thoughts. "Of course, I am. Why would you even ask that?"

Gwen's eyes drifted to the room over Eloise's shoulder. "It's just that you've chosen a life that's so different from the one you grew up in. The one you were told to expect to live. I hope you're ready for what lies ahead."

In an instant Eloise was back in the courtyard that night when she'd first met Tuck, when everything had begun, and just as clearly as she could picture that night, she could remember how she had felt.

Trapped.

All the things she had ever wished for were suddenly gone when the expectations of reality had descended upon her. But all of that had changed now. Changed because she'd made a different choice, one for only herself.

She smiled. "I've been waiting for this the whole of my life."

Gwen laughed, kissed her sister on the cheek and left, calling behind her, "Don't forget dinner."

* * *

Tuck had told Eloise he had a meeting at the Royal Astronomical Society, but that was, in fact, a lie.

One week married, and he was already lying to his wife. Did that foreshadow terrible things to come? He thought not. Especially because the lie had everything to do with their future and securing their happiness.

It was odd having to knock on his cousin's door. He was always so used to walking in, feeling as though the place were his home too. But that no longer felt right. Instead, he felt like a trespasser.

"Do not tell me you do me the disservice of knocking on the door, cousin?"

Tuck looked around as if his thoughts had somehow materialized, but when he turned about he found Liam standing at the bottom of the stairs behind him.

"Cousin," he said, but Liam's scowl didn't lessen.

"Are you knocking on my door or are you not?"

Tuck straightened his shoulders and said what he'd come here to say. "I've come to apologize for stealing your wife. If you wish to never speak to me again, I shall understand."

Of all the things he expected Liam to do, what he did do was not one of them.

He laughed.

He laughed so much Tuck feared he'd have a stroke and die right there on the pavement. He laughed so much he doubled over, a hand to his stomach. He laughed so much tears came to his eyes.

Tuck stared. "Is my apology so amusing to you then?"

When Liam finally managed to wipe away his tears with the back of his hand, he climbed the stairs two at a time. "You'd better come inside," he said, sailing past his cousin.

Tuck felt mildly relieved when he realized it did feel like coming home, stepping inside the foyer of Ardley House. The familiar marble floors contrasting with the dark woodworking felt like a cocoon ready to pull him in, and for a second, he forgot his cousin's unusual response to his apology.

For only a second though.

Liam strode directly through the house to the study at the back where he tossed aside his riding gloves and hat before going to the bell pull in the corner.

"I think we should have sustenance for this. Have you broken your fast?" He turned back to Tuck after giving the cord a pull. "I can have something more substantial brought up."

Tuck could only shake his head, unsure of what was happening. He'd come here to apologize, and his cousin offered him breakfast.

"I'm fine. Liam, I hope you don't think I'm ungrateful for what you've done."

Liam's eyebrows knitted together in a look of wary concentration Tuck had never seen on his cousin's face before. He almost looked…guilty.

"Say nothing of it, cousin," Liam said, going over to his desk to discard his jacket and then—

Dear Lord, Liam rolled up the sleeves of his shirt. Just what exactly did he plan to have transpire here?

"You should take a seat," Liam said.

Tuck sat. He was lucky a sofa was behind him because just then he really wasn't looking. He could only stare at his cousin.

Liam made his way over and sat next to him on the sofa, and for one absurd moment, Tuck felt as though he'd left his body. For surely he must have. He still wore his hat and coat, but he was far closer to a debutante just then waiting for her beau to ask for permission to write her. This entire thing was madness.

"Tuck, you know I think of you as family," Liam began.

"I'm your cousin," Tuck muttered.

Liam waved this off. "You know what I mean. I think of you as a brother." He paused, but Tuck knew not to cut in. Liam was only gathering steam. "And as your honorary brother, it is my responsibility to ensure your future happiness and health."

"What in the name of Zeus are you talking about?"

"I meddled."

At first, Tuck couldn't understand what his cousin had just said. Liam had all but murmured the words, but even then, Tuck couldn't make sense of them.

"You meddled?"

"I did. But I want you to know it was for your own good." Liam held up a finger as if to enumerate his points, but instead, he said, "If you wish for me to apologize, I shall, but I want you to know I would commit the same actions again." He cast his eyes toward the ceiling as if thinking it over. "Actually I would have done it better. I can see now where missteps were made." He dropped his gaze. "But some things happened in a spectacular fashion I never could have counted on. Like that incident with the dog? Splendid. Had no idea it would occur." He shook his head, his eyes wide, a satisfied grin plastered across his face.

"Liam, I think you'd better explain."

Liam's expression faded. "I never intended to marry Lady Eloise."

Tuck surged to his feet, his shock propelling him off the sofa. "You what?"

Liam stood too, holding out his hands as if in surrender. "I never intended to marry Eloise. I apologize for misleading you, but I couldn't think of another way to force you to act."

"Force me to act?" Tuck made to run his hand through his hair when it connected with his hat, sending the thing flying. He didn't stop to pick it up. "What are you talking about, Liam? I didn't come to London for a wife."

"I know. That's precisely the problem." Liam spoke so softly it had the fire burning inside of Tuck cooling. His cousin only used that tone when he was truly serious.

"What do you mean by that?" Tuck asked.

But Liam was prevented from speaking by the arrival of a maid with a tea cart. She paused ever so slightly just over the threshold as if she could sense the tension in the room. Liam smiled and bade her enter. She remained skeptical the entire time she laid out the tea on the low table in front of the sofa.

The moment the door closed behind her, Tuck rounded on his cousin. "Explain yourself."

Liam sat and began to pour tea as if he hadn't just revealed that it was, in fact, he who was the betraying cousin.

"I would just like to point out that Lady Eloise was at the top of my list for potential suitors." Liam looked up from where he was shoveling sugar into his own cup. "You must admit she would have made a remarkable duchess."

"Must I?" Tuck all but growled.

It looked as if Liam couldn't stop his smile. "Ah, I see. I am once more glad I meddled."

"Get on with it, cousin," Tuck prodded.

"Right, of course." He went back to shoveling sugar. "I had intentions of learning more about Lady Eloise Bounds as she did meet many of my criteria for a wife, and I thought she would make an excellent duchess and companion." He held out another cup of tea to Tuck, but Tuck shook his head. Liam frowned. "You must, cousin. You've had a shock, and your body will appreciate the sugar."

Tuck knew him to be right, but he didn't like it. Taking the cup, he sat none too gently on an opposite chair and reclined, ready to glower his cousin to death.

"Now then. I had vetted Lady Eloise as I had the rest of the candidates." He looked up from where he was selecting biscuits from a bone China plate. "You do understand that is common practice? I shan't wish you to think I considered your wife to be something of a piece of horseflesh."

Tuck merely waved for him to go on.

"But that first night after you arrived when we attended the Thornton ball—" He stopped in his selection of cream tarts to look at Tuck. "You may not realize this, but while Lady Eloise was being introduced I was actually watching you. The moment she appeared behind her mother you went preternaturally still. I worried you were having a medical issue it was so unnatural. But no. I was wrong. It wasn't medical. It was romantic. You recognized Lady Eloise." Liam sat back on the sofa with his array of sweets. "Care to tell me how it is you knew a lady of the *ton* at your first social function in London?"

Tuck took a long sip of his tea, letting it burn its way down his throat. He had come to Ardley House that morning ready to tell all, but this wasn't quite what he had meant by such thinking.

"I accidentally came upon her the night before that ball," he said, finding his voice catching on the last word, knowing it to be not quite the truth.

Liam paused with a petit four halfway to his mouth. "And how exactly did that occur?"

Tuck nodded in the direction of the windows that overlooked the shared courtyard. "Just out there actually. I'd gone out to test my stargazing spectacles."

Liam leaned forward, setting down his petit four unfinished. "Stargazing?" He looked about as if he'd lost something. "Well, I should think stargazing might occur at quite a later hour. Did you say it was evening when you encountered Lady Eloise?"

Tuck pushed the hair off his forehead. "Well, it might have been later than that, yes."

"How much later?" Liam's tone remained unchanged.

"Middle of the night perhaps." Tuck took some pleasure in watching Liam try to remain composed.

"Middle of the—" Liam was forced to stop and clear his throat. Likely the laughter he was attempting to contain was getting in the way of his speech. "Middle of the night? How interesting. I say, what was a lady like Eloise doing out in the courtyard in the middle of the night?"

"I couldn't say," Tuck replied.

Liam shrugged. "Well, I suppose that was an unusually romantic way to meet a person for the first time."

"She thought I was a ghoul."

Liam's eyebrows shot up. "A what?"

"A ghoul." Tuck tapped a finger to his temple. "I had the railway spectacles on. The ones I had outfitted with red glass."

Liam's tone was dire. "You didn't."

"I did."

His cousin pinched the bridge of his nose with two fingers. "Then it is lucky I intervened."

Tuck sat up, remembering he was not the one on trial here. "Speaking of which, how exactly did you intervene?"

Liam dropped his hand and met Tuck's gaze. "If you think it was I who locked you two in that broom cupboard, there's something I must admit." Tuck waited, holding his breath. "I'm utterly annoyed it wasn't me who thought of it." He slapped his thigh with one hand. "What a damn fine idea. Wish I had come up with it myself." Tuck could only frown. Liam gyrated his eyebrows annoyingly. "It really did the trick, which was good because I was running out of excuses to get the two of you together." He shook his head and returned to his petit fours. "You're a difficult man to convince of his own happiness, Tuck. I was reaching depletion."

Tuck frowned. "Trust me when I say I was well aware of it. It was only my loyalty to you that got in the way."

Liam swallowed the bit of sweet. "Loyalty to me? God, what had that to do with it?"

Tuck leaned forward, elbows to knees. "I thought you were going to marry her. What we did—" He stopped, realizing what he had been about to reveal in his annoyance. "It was betrayal, Liam. I've been carrying that around for months now. I probably have a stomach ailment." He rubbed at his stomach for greater effect.

Liam only laughed. "Is that what was holding you back?" He slapped his thigh again. "Damn. I wish I had known. Would have saved me a great deal of trouble." He reached for the plate of eclairs and held it up. "Can I offer you an eclair as recompense?"

"You're lucky I care a great deal for you," Tuck muttered.

Liam smiled. "It's almost like we're family."

CHAPTER 12

After moving the kitchen linens three times, Eloise decided it was time to do something about the thoughts rattling around in her head.

She was walking through the front gate of the Stoke Bruerne home before she could change her mind. She'd waited a week already to have this conversation with her mother, and a week was entirely too long. She must stop being a ninny and face the truth.

She'd ruined every last expectation her mother held for her, and now Eloise must bear the consequences.

The only shred of hope remaining was what Gwen had said about her debut season. Was it true that their mother had wanted a season for Gwen? That her only desire was to see her daughters find matches, companions that would accompany them for all the rest of their lives?

Nancy Bounds just wasn't that practical. Surely Gwen had it wrong.

But what if she didn't?

What if Eloise had allowed the start of her marriage to be ever so slightly tarnished by a misunderstanding?

She plowed on through the front door, not bothering to shed her gloves and hat and went directly to the south drawing room where she knew her mother and grandmother would likely be at this hour. Startling a maid in the process, she swept down the corridor, dodging a footman who had the terrible timing of coming up the servants' stairs at the exact moment she passed the door.

The drawing room doors were flung wide when she reached them, and voices drifted into the hallway. Eloise rounded the corner, her speech ready on her lips, when—

She froze.

Somewhere in the back of her mind, she had anticipated finding the usual tableau one might find in the south drawing room at this hour. Grandmother Bitsy by the fire, no matter the time of year, quietly knitting and unraveling the same skein of yarn. Eloise's mother would be nestled in the bay windows on the opposite side of the room, the day's invitations spread on her lap while she poured over them like a general constructing her battle plans.

But that was not what was occurring in the drawing room.

For one, the furniture had all been pushed aside to make room for a table Eloise was certain had once lived in the library. It was the wide rectangular one at which she'd learned her numbers when she was quite young, and Gwen and Annie had tried to make her lose her place by speaking out loud other numbers to distract her.

On this table was a mess of papers, newspapers, stacks of books, books thrown open and discarded, ink bottles, quills, and—was that a half-eaten sandwich?

Her mother leaned over the table on one side while Grandmother Bitsy perched on a chair at the opposite end, holding a newspaper so close to her face she couldn't possibly see anything.

"I've gone through the papers from last week, but we'll want to check the ones from the week before. Some of these things take time, and the first sign of them may be further back than we think," Nancy said, shuffling through the stack of papers in front of her. She collided with the half-eaten sandwich and tossed it aside without pause.

Eloise cleared her throat. "Mother?"

Nancy looked up, blinking as if to clear sleep from her eyes, and it was several seconds before a smile came to her lips, recognition registering in her gaze. "Eloise. Wonderful. You can start on the correspondence from the twenty-fifth." Her mother held out a bundle of what appeared to be invitations wrapped in a pale blue ribbon.

Eloise didn't move but instead addressed her grandmother. "I'm sorry. I don't know what's happening."

Grandmother Bitsy didn't move the paper from her nose. "We're at war, dear. It's best you take a chair. This might take a great deal of time."

Eloise made her way slowly over to the table and took the bundle from her mother for fear the woman would continue to hold her hand out like that for eternity if Eloise didn't take it.

"I don't understand. Is this about Viscountess Bowes?" Eloise asked, her eyes drifting between her grandmother, mother, and even the half-eaten sandwich.

"Viscountess Bowes?" Her mother blinked rapidly again as if trying to comprehend. "What has she to do with this?" Her mother set down the stack of papers she'd been going through with a huff. "Why? What have you heard? Has something happened?" She pointed a finger accusingly at Eloise. "Is it her youngest? Did she make a match?" Before Eloise could respond, Nancy scoffed and looked away. "Absurd. The girl is hardly out of the schoolroom."

"Mother," Eloise cut in, afraid her mother would launch

into her list of reasons why Viscountess Bowes was the vilest woman in London. "I'm not here about Viscountess Bowes. I've come here to apologize."

Her mother took a step back, her mouth opening in surprise. "Apologize? Whatever for?"

"For not marrying Ardley."

Her mother blinked again, and Eloise grew concerned her mother was developing a nerve disorder. "Bitsy, do you know what she's talking about?" Nancy turned her gaze to Grandmother Bitsy who had picked up the half-eaten sandwich and was sniffing it suspiciously. She only shook her head, and Nancy turned her attention back to Eloise. "What are you talking about, dear?"

Eloise stepped up to the table and gripped the edge as if it might help get her through this. "I know you wanted me to marry Ardley, and I'm sorry I wasn't able to live up to your expectations. I hope—" She licked her lips and swallowed. "I hope I haven't disappointed you too much." Eloise was surprised to find tears clogging her voice, and she held her breath to stop them from falling.

Her mother dropped the remaining papers in her hand and strode around the table, her arms outstretched. "Eloise, darling, you mustn't apologize." When her mother's arms closed around her, tears did come to her eyes then, but she held herself still as if that could prevent her mother from seeing them. Her mother loosened her grip but didn't let go of Eloise as she said, "You've never disappointed me, little one."

Eloise was startled by her mother's use of the nickname she hadn't used since Eloise was a small child. It was as though those two words stopped her tears completely, and she stared at her mother.

"I'm absolutely thrilled that you found someone you care about as much as you care about Tuck. He is a good man, and he will care for you, and that is all I could ever hope for for my daughters. Don't you know that?"

"But you wanted us to catch the dukes," Eloise managed.

Her mother laughed. "Oh, but Annie did catch a duke. A duke she loves very much, and one who, I think, makes her happy. She's wearing colors again, haven't you noticed?" Her mother sighed and shook her head. "I don't know how I got so lucky." She moved back then and took Eloise's shoulders in her hands and gave her an encouraging shake. "And now you. Tuck is simply marvelous, and I think he makes you happy. Doesn't he?" Her mother's brow furrowed for a moment. "If he doesn't make you happy, say the word, and I'll have it taken care of."

Her voice had turned so dramatically ominous Eloise laughed. "Oh no, he makes me very happy, Mother, but…he's not a duke."

"So?" her mother asked, one eyebrow going up. "He loves you, and you love him, and you've promised to support each other and be there for each other." Her mother shrugged. "What else matters?"

Eloise stared. "Gwen said you wouldn't care that he wasn't a duke."

"When did Gwen say that?"

"She came to see me earlier. She wanted to—" Again Eloise's throat closed on the words. "She wanted to tell me I should speak to you because I thought I might have disappointed you."

Her mother's laugh was rich. "Oh little one, you couldn't be further from the truth." She sobered, her eyes moving aside as if thinking about something. "Terrified me? Yes. Made me rethink my decision to have a third child? Yes." She looked back at Eloise. "But never disappointed. Never."

"But we didn't get both dukes," Eloise whispered.

Her mother waved a hand and started back around the

table. "What does it matter? I managed to marry off all three of my daughters in a single season, and Rosemary hasn't received a single offer for one of hers." Her mother threw up her hands in triumph. "I am victorious!"

Eloise couldn't help but smile at her mother's obvious glee even if it were at the expense of another person. She gestured to the table.

"Then what is all of this about?"

Nancy glanced over the detritus scattered across the table. "Oh, this. This is for Tuck."

It was Eloise's turn to blink. "For Tuck?"

"We're looking for money, shortcake," Grandmother Bitsy said from behind a week-old copy of *The Gazette*. "So you two can go to the North Pole."

"Money?"

Her mother nodded, scooping up a stack of papers and moving them aside. "In here, we will find the funds Tuck needs for his expedition." Her mother tapped another bundle of old invitations. "We only must find the patterns. Between announcements, stories covering business transactions, and invitations, we'll find who has money they're looking to invest." Her mother met Eloise's gaze. "Things aren't like they used to be. Everything is about business now, and somewhere in this mess is our answer. We only must find it."

Eloise considered the bundle she'd taken from her mother. "You would do all of this? For Tuck?"

"Of course, I would," her mother said quickly.

"I plan to go with him, Mother," Eloise said in a rush. "I plan to go with him to Spitsbergen."

"I know," her mother said.

"You know?" This conversation was getting stranger by the second.

"I wouldn't expect anything else from you," her mother said, straightening a pile of books.

"But it means I'll be gone for many months. I don't know if your letters will even reach me. And—"

"Eloise, dear," her mother interjected, her tone practical. "What kind of mother would I be if I hadn't prepared you to fly the nest?" She shook her head. "Do you know how proud I am of you for embarking on this life? Your accomplishments reflect on me as a mother, Eloise. Don't you know that?" Her mother held out both hands as if to show off Eloise in some way. "And look at you. I would say I did a marvelous job of it. Wouldn't you, Bitsy?"

Grandmother Bitsy peered around the edge of the paper. "With this one, yes. I am choosing to withhold my judgment on the other two." She disappeared back behind the newsprint.

Eloise laughed, the only thing she was capable of then as her world seemed to tilt around her, trying to find its new positioning.

"Well then, I suppose I should get started," Eloise said, setting the bundle down long enough to strip off her gloves and unpin her hat.

She had just set her outer things aside when rapid footsteps in the corridor drew her attention.

"Father," she said, her surprise noticeable in her voice as the Earl Stoke Bruerne swept into the room, his arms full of—

Newspapers.

Eloise's heart tripped.

"I've got all the afternoon editions with the exception of *The Chronicle.*" He dropped the lot of it with a thud in the middle of the table. "They ran a story on that Shepard's affair. Apparently copies sold out in minutes. But I think this should be enough to get us started." He shrugged out of his coat then and rolled up his sleeves before taking the newspaper from the top of the pile.

Eloise stared. She'd never in her life seen her father's forearms.

She reached out and touched his shoulder. "Thank you, Papa," she said.

He only made a gruff noise of acknowledgment and disappeared behind his paper.

* * *

"HE WHAT?" Eloise sat with a huff at the small table in the kitchen portion of their rented rooms.

She was surprised to have arrived home that afternoon to find their home empty, but now that her husband had launched into his explanation of where he'd been, she understood what had kept him away.

"Ardley really had no intention of asking me to marry him?" She didn't know why she was offended by this. It wasn't as though she had wished to marry the man. In fact, that had been precisely the problem. But to hear he hadn't wished to marry her? Well, that was ridiculous. She was a catch. Any marrying mama could have told him that.

Tuck eyed her quizzically from where he sat opposite her at their little table. "You can call him Liam now. He is your cousin after all."

She stared. "I can only think of him as Ardley. It would be terribly strange to call him anything else."

He shrugged. "Perhaps you'll feel better about it when we return from Spitsbergen next spring."

His words reminded her why she'd been out that day, and she got to her feet to find her bag.

"Does the idea of calling him Liam trouble you so?" Tuck called after her as she raced to find the notes she'd brought home with her.

When she got back to the table, she spread out the sheets of paper that were the result of their day's work.

She tapped them with one finger. "A list of potential benefactors." She indicated the name at the top. "They go in order of most likely to fund the expedition to least likely but still not without potential."

He studied the sheet, but it didn't appear as though he was truly absorbing what they'd done.

This became clear when he said, "I don't understand."

She pushed her chair closer to his. "I went to visit my mother today," she began and told him what had occurred when she'd found her family in the drawing room sketching battle plans.

He sat back when she'd finished explaining the list between them. "Your mother didn't actually want you to marry a duke?"

She shrugged. "I suppose she did in some way but not in the way I had believed. It was more that she wanted me to be safe and cared for and most importantly loved." She picked at a scar on the table's surface much as she had when Gwen had been there that morning. Lud, had so much really happened in a single day? It seemed entirely unlikely, but there it was. "I guess I never realized how much in love my parents are." She met her husband's gaze. "My father's been behind a newspaper for most of my life. It was really quite surprising how he came up to snuff when needed."

There was a smile on his face then that reminded her of that first night in the courtyard, boyish and happy, and her heart clenched with hope. It was a funny flutter in her chest, and she realized she hadn't felt hope since their first engagement of the season when she'd realized the truth of the man who had captured her heart under the stars.

That man laid his hand on hers now, stilling her anxious

movements. "I think your parents love you a great deal and want to see you happy."

She couldn't help but laugh at this. "Happy isn't always safe. I'm rather concerned at how readily they were willing to send me north of the Arctic Circle." She wrinkled her nose. "I could get eaten by polar bears, and I'm not sure they even care."

He laughed, more heartily than she thought warranted, and she eyed him.

"Liam is worried about any polar bear that might encounter you. He's afraid the victor in that match might not be the animal."

She pulled her hand from under his, feigning hurt. "Of all the nerve. As if I would hurt a polar bear." She paused for emphasis. "I would give the creature ample time to leave before I did anything."

He smiled, but it quickly faded as he glanced back down at the paper in front of him. "Your family was very kind to do this, but..." He met her gaze. "I haven't been very successful in obtaining a benefactor. It's the having to speak to them that trips me up."

She took his hand in hers. "But you have me now. I'll do the speaking, and you provide the facts. It will work out perfectly."

He didn't seem assured, but he asked, "Where shall we start?"

She let go of him to pick up the envelope that she'd found shoved under their door when she'd returned from Stoke Bruerne House earlier.

"With the Earl of Renshaw," she said, handing him the envelope.

Taking it from her, he frowned. "But the earl has no money."

"I know," she said. "But he's invited us to dinner."

"I thought you said this was a dinner," Tuck murmured, looking about the room. "We're the only ones here."

Tuck took in the drawing room where they'd been brought. It was a room he had never seen in all of his visits to the earl. It was a small room with oppressively heavy green velvet drapes at the window, a set of chairs before a fireplace that appeared never to have been used, and a faded and careworn carpet across the floor. That was it. There wasn't another piece of furniture in the room, and the whole space reeked of dust.

Eloise stepped closer to him. "Are you certain the earl isn't really a mad totter?"

He shrugged. "He's never seemed mad the many times I've spoken to him."

She gave him a glance that suggested she didn't quite believe him and remained by his side while they waited.

And waited.

And waited some more.

Unlike the other times he had been there, the house was

silent around them. It made the tick of the clock above the fireplace sound louder than it actually was, echoing in the quiet that blanketed them.

A quarter of an hour past and then another.

Eloise shifted from foot to foot. "Do you think we should go look for someone?" She clutched his arm and leaned forward, bringing up one foot, wriggling her toes, and switching to the other. "These shoes are not meant to be stood in."

He watched her repeat the movements several times. "Then why on earth are you wearing them?"

She blinked, appearing slightly hurt. "Because they're cute."

When the footsteps sounded in the hall, they both jumped, so startling was the sound in the unending silence.

The earl himself appeared in the doorway. Well, at least his head did.

"Oh, there you are," he said before stepping fully into the doorway. He looked around much as Tuck had done. "I didn't even know this room was here." He made a noise of appreciation then and looked to where Tuck and Eloise waited. "I bet you two are starving. Come, come. We mustn't tarry any longer. I believe Cook has prepared a feast."

Tuck was relieved to see the earl wore pants. Although they were purple, and his dinner jacket was peach. He had all the other requisite pieces of clothing in place, however, and Tuck took Eloise's arm as they followed the earl into the hall.

If Tuck had his bearings correct, the earl was taking them back to the library where Tuck had met with him every time he'd come to visit the earl. The library was a strange place to have dinner, but then perhaps the earl preferred a drink before the meal.

Except when they stepped into the library, it was to find a circular table laid for dinner.

A table that sat a scant two feet above the floor and was surrounded by cushions. The surface of it was laid with an intricately woven cloth bursting with bright colors—reds, oranges, and turquoise. Strewn across its surface were flower petals, roses it looked it. There were three empty plates set at intervals around its circumference, and that was all.

Tuck wasn't sure which one of them stopped first, but their elbows locked together like a chain.

Tippy loped around the table, sweeping a hand grandly over it. "Sit, sit. I hope you are adventurous eaters. I thought a nice Moroccan meal was in order." He took a seat then. That is, to say, he flounced down on the floor against the pile of cushions on the other side of the table.

Tuck swallowed and turned to his wife to gage her reaction. He wasn't surprised to find her beaming.

She tugged her arm free and without hesitation pulled up her skirts before settling onto another cushion pile.

"Moroccan, you say?" Eloise adjusted her skirts.

Tuck thought Tippy's smile might rival his wife's. "Oh yes," he said. "My Carolina and I spent a wonderful three days trapped in Tafraoute. Blocked in by a sandstorm. The innkeeper there took pity on us and treated us to a feast." Tippy leaned forward, resting his chin in the cup of his palm as he planted one elbow on the table. "What a wonderful feast that was," he murmured dreamily before straightening with bright eyes. "The innkeeper was the great nephew of the sultan, you see, and had the connections to get all the best meat there was to be had. Never had a tagine like it since." He sat up and shook his head, his gaze somewhere else as if he were recalling the very taste of the meal.

Tuck took the remaining seat at the table, feeling as though the world about him had shifted. Was the earl really the mad totter everyone thought him to be? He glanced at Eloise, but she was smiling wistfully at the earl.

Tippy shook his head and straightened just as two footmen entered carrying platters of food. Tuck leaned back from the table, expecting to be served, but the footmen simply placed the platters in the middle of the table, bowed, and withdrew.

This wasn't the end of the oddness, however. Tippy sat up and without ceremony scooped a helping of vegetables from one platter, a variety of tomatoes and aubergines and something else Tuck couldn't identify. He scooped it with his bare hand.

"I grow all the vegetables in my own garden, you see. Can't very well trust to get fresh ones from abroad, now can we?" He looked up, a gleam in his eye. "Perhaps one day though, eh, Tuck? Can you imagine? Fresh fruits and vegetables from around the world delivered to your kitchen before they spoil?" He shook his head. "Now that's a fantasy." He gestured to Eloise. "You use your hands in Moroccan culture, my dear. Eat always with your right and save your left hand for when you need a clean one."

Tuck stared at his beautiful wife, Lady Eloise Bounds, whom he had married beyond everything that said they shouldn't be wed.

She leaned forward too and scooped a handful of the vegetable mixture onto her plate. "And how long were you in Morocco, my lord?"

Tippy waved a hand, his clean one as a matter of fact. "Please, dear, the name is Tippy. And my Carolina wanted to languish in Morocco forever, but we had business to attend to in Peru."

Tuck blinked. What was going on here? He'd come to know the earl quite well in the past few weeks. He'd visited the man with some kind of regularity and learned he preferred Scottish shortbread to chocolate biscuits, a warm fire and a rug over his lap with a good book at night, and when he was feeling particularly wild, a walk in Hyde Park.

But this…

Morocco?

Peru?

"What took you to Peru?" Eloise asked the question while Tuck scooped up his own serving.

"Ah, that would be our guano business." Tippy looked between them. "You both are aware of the use of bat dung as a fertilizer, I take it?"

Tuck blinked. "I'm afraid I'm not familiar with the practice."

Tippy nodded. "Yes, it's rather a niche business but profitable. My Carolina always did have a head for business. That's why I took her suggestion that we invest in guano with her dowry. It turned out she was right." Again the shake of his head, but this time it was almost whimsical. "She was always right," he said more softly now.

"And you took an active role in your…" Eloise swallowed. "Guano investment?"

Tippy looked up, eyes widening as though he had forgotten he had guests for dinner. "Oh, yes." Another shake of the head. "Well, no, it wasn't an investment like that, really. It was a business. Carolina and I ran it together, you see, and now I have a board of directors who oversee it." He sat back. "That's why I asked you both to dinner actually. I hope you don't mind talking of business over a meal, but I've never seen the purpose in such formality." He shrugged. "I'd like to leave my business to the two of you. To fund your future expeditions."

Eloise held a piece of tomato and aubergine between two fingers as though she had meant to take a bite but had been frozen by Tippy's words. Tuck hadn't been able to touch a morsel as their strange conversation unfolded, so he simply sat there, staring.

"I've already set it all up, so I hope you don't turn me down." Tippy laughed good-naturedly. "The directors will continue to oversee the business, and any profits will be deposited into the account marked for your expeditions. You can do with the funds what you will, of course. While I have a taste for adventure and a spirit for the unknown, I can't say I'm especially educated in the matter of science." He paused then, a look of almost impossible hope coming into his eyes. "I hope you'll indulge me once in a while and tell me what it is you're finding up there in the north." He paused again, as if considering his own words. "Well, for as long as I'm still on this plane. Before I go see my Carolina again." His face split into a grin.

Tuck could not speak.

Luckily, Eloise still held her wits. "Tippy, are you saying you're…"

"Bloody rich," Tippy said. "No one knows, of course. Except for you two and my directors." He wrinkled his nose. "My peers tend to frown upon wealth which stems from the steaming piles of bat dung, and so I never told them about it." He shrugged and went back to his meal. "Their loss really. I could have saved many a fortune if any of them had listened to me." He tucked into his meal as if he hadn't just changed the course of their lives forever.

"Excuse me." Tuck finally found his voice. "You're telling me you're going to fund my expedition to Spitsbergen?" He was forced to ask the question in the simplest of terms because everything seemed so befuddled now.

Tippy nodded. "Spitsbergen and beyond, of course. Wherever your research should take you." He shook his head and made an encouraging noise as if imagining the future. "There's a stipend for you to live on, of course. You'll need moneys for lodging, food, and clothing." He named a sum then that was four times what Tuck took in a year between his teaching and the allowance from his father.

Four times.

Tuck made enough to support the two of them in a reasonable fashion. They would be required to adhere to a tight budget, but they would never starve. But four times that amount…well, they would live like kings.

It was a good thing Tuck was sitting on the floor already, or he might have collapsed.

"My lord, I mean Tippy…" But Eloise didn't say anything else, and quite frankly, Tuck couldn't have either.

Tippy nodded though as if Eloise had actually said something of substance. "I know, but the thing is I see in the two of you a kindred spirit." He waved a single finger at them. "My decision was cemented the moment Bitsy told me you were to wed." He looked at Tuck then, his expression suddenly grave. "I had planned to fund your expedition no matter what, but when I heard you were to have a companion on your travels, well…" He shrugged. "It made me nostalgic, I guess, and there was nothing I could do except make you my heir."

Eloise's hand at his back was the only way Tuck knew he had swayed backward at Tippy's announcement. "Heir?"

"Well, the title will go to some cousin, I think." He looked to the ceiling. "A watery chap in Devonshire, if I remember correctly. Has an unusual obsession with hair pomade." He shook his head and looked back to the two of them. "What can one do. But the business is mine, of course, and you shall have it upon my death. Do with it as you please but take heed." He leaned forward, elbow on the table as if to emphasize his point. "There's good money in bat dung."

The door behind Tuck opened, and a parade of elephants pirouetting through a ballet might have come through for all he could understand. But it wasn't. It was just the same pair of footmen. This time they carried clay pots that emitted the aroma of onions, tomatoes, and parsley.

"Ah, the main course, splendid." Tippy waited until the footmen had placed the clay pots on the table and left before he eyed the two of them. "Now that business is out of the way, I should love to tell the story of how Carolina and I almost died from an illness we contracted in a cave."

"Where was the cave? Dartmoor?" Tuck heard himself say although he couldn't have said where he'd summoned the words from.

Tippy laughed heartily. "Oh no, son. It was in the Tayos Caves of Ecuador," he whispered, his voice dropping low, pulling them both into his tale.

And so Tuck ate while sitting on the floor next to the wife he still couldn't believe he had while he listened to the adventurous tales of the man who had just made Tuck bloody rich.

* * *

Some hours later they lay in the dark on the sagging bed of their rented rooms. They didn't speak, and they didn't touch. They simply lay there, next to each other, man and wife, two people whose entire future had changed so abruptly and then abruptly again in the space of only weeks.

"Tuck?" Eloise finally ventured. "Are you...all right?"

It seemed such a horribly inadequate thing to say. This was his entire life's work practically presented to him on a platter.

He didn't speak, but she heard his hair rustle against his pillow as he nodded.

The silence grew until it acquired a sound, a low buzzing in her ears. She heard the clip clop of a horse on the street outside. It was probably a hackney carrying home a late-night reveler. There was the settling of the building, the faint moan and creak of an old edifice relaxing into its joints as the temperature dropped. It was a strange sound that had grown familiar over the past weeks they'd lived in their rented rooms, and now it brought her comfort.

Finally she sat up, pushing herself up against the headboard and moving her braid of hair over her shoulder so it no longer tickled her face.

"I can't believe the Earl of Renshaw is wealthy," she whispered as if she were afraid to speak it out loud. She let her gaze linger on the thin curtains at the window, the shape of the building beside theirs nearly visible through them. "He would always bring each of us a daisy he plucked from his own garden when he came to visit Grandmother Bitsy when we were children. We thought it the most generous gift from a doting old man." She turned to where Tuck was a shadow on the bed beside her. "How he must miss his wife. Heavens, it almost hurts to take his money."

It was nearly midnight when they'd left Tippy. He'd seen them to the door himself and waited on the stoop until they were safely in his carriage. He'd insisted on them taking it to see their way home, and they'd found they simply couldn't refuse his generosity. Not after hearing the stories of his adventurous life with his beloved Carolina.

Finally Tuck showed the first signs of life since they'd returned to their rented rooms. He pushed himself to a seated position much like her and rested his head against the wall behind the bed.

"I think it means something to him, to give us his fortune." He didn't look at her. His eyes lingered on the thin curtains much like hers had. "I think it's his way of making sure his wife lives on."

"By giving it to your expedition?"

He turned only his head, his eyes meeting hers. "By making sure the fortune she helped grow is used for something she loved."

She had no response to that and let her gaze travel back to the curtains.

It was only a minute later when he took her hand, startling her. She met his gaze.

"I'm feeling…scared," he said, his words hesitant to emerge. "This entire time the expedition to Spitsbergen has been a solitary thing, existing only in my mind, and then when I pictured the actual journey, it was just me alone." He held her hand in one of his, and with the other, he traced each of her fingers, circling knuckle and outlining each curve. "And now I have the funding needed to make the expedition happen, and suddenly it's real. All of it is real." He shook his head, his eyes dropping to where he traced her fingers. "And there's you." He paused, but he didn't look back up. He closed his other hand over hers before he looked at her. "I'm scared, Eloise. This thing that I imagined—" He shook his head, licked his lips nervously. "It's really happening. I'm going to Spitsbergen to study the aurora. To better understand solar flares and how they can affect us. I didn't think it would ever happen, and now I wonder if I'll be up to the task." He swallowed then, and somehow she knew that what he would say next was what truly plagued him. She wasn't surprised when he said, "If I'll be up to the task of ensuring Harrison's death wasn't meaningless."

She placed her hand over his. "Do you remember that night we first met?"

"When you thought I was a ghoul?" His voice had firmed a little, not sounding quite as lost, and she let that urge her on.

"Yes, a ghoul," she confirmed. "But when I understood you weren't a ghoul, do you know what I thought?"

He shook his head.

"I'd never met anyone as clever as you." He opened his lips, but she held up a single finger to stop him. "Smart? Yes, of course. I've met many a smart person in my little life. But not clever. There's a difference, you know."

"How's that?" A line had appeared between his brows.

"A smart person can know things. All manner of things really. But a clever person is one who can enact change. They do something with their knowledge."

The concern in his expression deepened. "And what did I do besides scare the devil out of you?"

"You took ordinary railway glasses and made them something else."

His expression blanked, but he didn't speak.

"Tell me I'm wrong. Did you not take something that existed, applied your understanding to it, and made it different?"

"I did do that," he said, but his tone was reluctant.

"It's evidence, Mr. Ryan," she said, scooting closer to him until she could cup his cheek and force his attention on her when he tried to move his gaze away. "Aren't you scientist types always concerned about the evidence?"

Now a weak smile came to his lips. "I suppose we are."

"And there's something else that you might not realize."

His eyes were more sure on hers now. "What's that?"

"You won't be doing this alone. You'll have me, and from now on, we do things together. Do you understand, Mr. Ryan?"

He placed his hand over the one that cupped his cheek, and his smile became certain. "I understand, Mrs. Ryan," he said before he kissed her.

It was on a sunny afternoon made even more beautiful by a gentle breeze that carried the scent of new blooms and cut grass that the Duke of Ardley finally met a woman who instantly fell in love with him.

Not for all his charms and his systemic way of winning a woman's affection.

No. He won her love by sitting down on the grass with her and letting her unravel his cravat.

Lady Felicity Bender was smitten within seconds.

She toddled over to the duke and threw her arms around his neck, gurgling happily when it was too much and telling him he was very pretty when she could form the words.

Eloise couldn't help but laugh along with the rest of the members of their little gathering.

It was a sendoff, but she didn't wish to think of it like that. She and Tuck were to leave within the fortnight for Spitsbergen, and everyone had gathered in the shared courtyard of Stoke Bruerne House. The supplies had all been purchased, guides hired for every leg of the expedition, and tickets in hand. It was time for them finally to go.

Eloise's mother had insisted on a formal gathering to give them a proper goodbye, and although it was hard to imagine leaving the only place she had ever known, there was too much excitement burbling within her to let any feelings of sadness or misgiving overtake her euphoria.

Gwen and Logan had made the trip down from Yorkshire with little Felicity. Eloise got to hold her for all of a minute before Grandmother Bitsy and Nancy had commandeered the poor child. But they both had lost to the duke, and Eloise found this fitting somehow. The man was nothing if not a strategist.

Gabriel fawned over Annie, and Eloise wondered if the man would make it through the entirety of Annie's pregnancy without expiring from the strain of it. They had wasted no time in starting their own little family, and even now, watching Gabriel bring Annie yet another glass of lemonade as she reclined in the shade—the poor woman was going to be using the retiring room all day—Eloise couldn't help but smile.

The only question was who would be delivered of their baby first. Eloise's eyes traveled to Gwen who sat next to her husband, her stomach already rounded enough to be straining her gown.

There was a pinch in her chest as she watched her sisters and their husbands, and Eloise wondered if she would meet these babes they carried. She shooed the thought away for the silliness that it was. Of course, she would meet them. They would return in the spring when the weather was favorable enough for travel, and then she would meet her new nieces or nephews or better yet perhaps there would be one of each.

Her eyes moved to Tuck then who was seated at the small table on the terrace with her father. They were debating over an editorial in *The Gazette* that asserted the platitudes of

Prime Minister Disraeli. Seeing Tuck sitting there, lounging so naturally, his speech so animated, Eloise wondered if he'd meant to be there all along, nestled here in the bosom of her family.

They'd traveled to Derbyshire for Eloise to meet Tuck's family and for them to wish them well on their journey. Eloise didn't know quite what she'd been expecting, but she wasn't surprised to find Tuck had been raised in a home full of books where a teapot was always at the ready and with a mother who while not demonstrably affectionate would likely raise an entire army to defend one of her children. It was the exact place where she wished to imagine little Tuck growing up.

Their visit was all too short, and they returned to London to find their expedition gear had been delivered to Tippy's. They'd given up their rented rooms after it became clear they were not large enough to house all of the equipment they were purchasing for the endeavor. Tippy had insisted they come live with him until it was time for them to depart, and they couldn't have thought of a better idea.

The earl gave his ideas on everything from the ropes they purchased to tie down the equipment to the dog sleds to the dried jerky they acquired for when fresh rations would run out. He plied them with stories of his and Carolina's adventures around the globe and gave them helpful warnings on what to avoid.

All of these warnings contained some story of bats in dark caves.

It had been a glorious couple of months, but the season was winding down, and with it, their departure drew near.

Eloise let her gaze drift over to Tippy who sat next to Grandmother Bitsy under the rose arbor. The two were deep in conversation, their voices hardly more than whispers.

She was startled when Tuck touched her shoulder as she'd been watching the pair in the arbor so intently.

Just before she turned to greet her husband, she caught Tippy sliding Grandmother Bitsy a coin.

"Grandmother," Eloise said, and the woman jumped as if caught. "Are you taking money from the earl?"

Tippy touched a hand dramatically to his forehead. "I'm afraid I'm helping her pay off her gambling debts." He glanced in Bitsy's direction. "We've been caught, my dear. Might as well give up."

Grandmother Bitsy stood with a sound of indignation. "I never give up, Tippy." She held the hand holding the coin to her chest. "And this is not gambling. It was a single wager, which I lost, and I've owed dear Hattie for some time. I'm a woman of honor, and I shall pay my debts accordingly."

"Hattie?" Eloise asked.

Grandmother Bitsy waved a hand in the air. "Lady Travers, child. I didn't think she'd get the two of you locked into that broom cupboard, and she not only managed the feat, but she acquired witnesses too."

Eloise shot to her feet. "*You* had us locked in that broom cupboard."

They had the attention of everyone in their little gathering then as Eloise was unable to control her voice, even when Tuck placed a calming hand on her shoulder.

Grandmother Bitsy scoffed as if offended. "I did no such thing." She shrugged as if it mattered very little. "I simply made a bet with Hattie that she couldn't see the deed done. I was wrong. She saw to it masterfully, and you two finally came to your senses and wed." She shook her head, her eyes wandering to the sky in frustration. "I must do everything around here."

Eloise and the rest of them had no choice but to watch

the woman walk away as she went to pay off her gambling debts.

CHAPTER 15

A *lifetime later...*

"WELL I, for one, don't see anything at all wrong with the situation."

Annette, their eldest daughter, turned to look at Eloise, her mouth slightly open in shock. "Mother, don't encourage her. No daughter of mine shall be found in a *flat* so she can engage in *employment* as a secretary."

"Annette, darling, if you sneer every word, they will lose all emphasis." Eloise cocked an eyebrow that only caused her daughter to gain her feet and march away in a huff, which was rather thwarted by the crowd that had jammed itself into the ballroom that evening.

Eloise watched her go even as her granddaughter, Annette's daughter, Gwendolyn, slid over to take her mother's vacated seat and gathered Eloise's hand into her own.

"Do you really feel that way, Grandmama?" Gwendolyn asked.

Eloise smiled as the light struck young Gwendolyn's eyes. They were the same color as her namesake, and looking into her granddaughter's gaze always reminded Eloise of her older sister, no matter how much distance now stood between them.

This Gwen had informed her family she intended to leave home and live on her own in a flat as she'd taken a position as a secretary in some industrialist company.

"I do believe it, Gwennie," she said, squeezing her granddaughter's hand. "Your grandfather and I lived in what you might call a flat when we were first wed."

Gwennie blinked, a smile lifting one side of her face. "You did? Was that before you left for Amsterdam?"

Eloise laughed, shaking her head. "Oh no, child. This was long before Amsterdam. Why your Uncle Harrison was already five by the time we left for Amsterdam. No, this was a great deal before that."

Gwennie sidled closer. "And did you love it? Living in a flat?"

Eloise laughed harder, whether at the memory or the eagerness in her granddaughter's gaze. "You must remember it was a different time then, and your grandfather and I had just been wed in scandal." She lowered her voice on the last word and wiggled her eyebrows for dramatic effect.

"Scandal?" Gwennie's eyes widened. She had her father's coloring, dark and earthy, and her wide eyes made her almost look like a specter.

"Of course, didn't your mother tell you?" Gwennie only shook her head, and Eloise made a tsking sound before saying, "That doesn't surprise me. Your mother always was a stickler for propriety. I'm sorry to say, young Gwennie, but Grandpapa and I were wed after we were discovered in a broom cupboard."

"What?"

This exclamation of astonishment came from the young man who had been in conversation at Eloise's elbow. He turned so swiftly a flop of light brown hair fell over his brow, and he looked so much like his grandfather just then it gave Eloise an actual pain in her chest.

"Oh Randall, surely you've heard this story."

Randall was Emma's son, their youngest daughter, and was studying chemistry in order to work with something called plastic. Eloise wasn't sure what was so interesting about it, but Tuck was always keen to catch up with Randall about his research when the boy had a break from his studies.

"I assure you I have not," he said, taking the seat beside her. "Why don't you enlighten both of us, Grandmama?"

"But you're missing the party," she said with a wave of her hand at the gathered guests. "You know parties aren't like they used to be. Back when I was your age, ballrooms were grand affairs." She flung a hand about her. "This is just two drawing rooms with a connecting door. As if no one would notice."

"How grand were they?" Gwennie prodded, but Eloise knew what she was really getting at.

"Well," she began. "You see, I wasn't supposed to marry your father. I was intended to marry a duke."

Randall's grin was more of a smirk, as if he were amusing his dear old grandmother. "Is that so, Grandmama? And who was this duke?"

Eloise waved him off. "Oh, it turns out he's not very central to our story. Let me explain."

She was nearly to the bit about Annie marrying Grimsby when a pair of shined and polished shoes stepped into her vision as she was attempting to recall what month it was when Annie married again. She looked up and into the face she'd been seeing every morning for more than sixty years.

"Darling, I was just telling the children how it was we met."

Both of Tuck's eyebrows, thoroughly gray now, rose up. "Surely you're not." He gestured behind him. "There's a party going on. With dancing and champagne and revelry. Why are you all sitting in this corner?"

Gwennie stood first and kissed her grandfather's cheek. "Grandmama was just telling us this wild story about how she was once promised to a duke." Gwennie shook her head. "Doesn't she tell the best stories?"

Tuck's smile was familiar and knowing, and it had Eloise smiling in return.

"Yes, she does tell the best stories, poppet."

Gwennie kissed his cheek again before pulling Randall up to go join a group of their friends by the bar.

Eloise was slower in getting to her feet. Her right knee had pained her ever since she'd slipped climbing that Alp, and it had never been quite right since. She wasn't sure which was more annoying, the fact that she'd done it or that if she'd done it at thirty-five instead of seventy-two it probably wouldn't still be paining her now. It was some kind of twisted blessing to grow so old as they had.

She wound her arm through her husband's and nodded at the crowd around them.

"Can you believe it, Mr. Ryan? We did all of this, you know."

Tuck laid his hand on hers and squeezed as they gazed over the room together, her head resting on his shoulder.

It was their granddaughter Ellen's engagement party. After Harrison and Annette had come Timothy and Sarah and finally Emma. Harrison had learned to read in a hut on Spitsbergen, and Annette had learned to tie her shoes when Tuck was on a lecture circuit through America. Timothy and Sarah had learned to ride horseback across the plains of

Africa, and Emma had learned three languages before she was five years old just so she could communicate with her nannies.

That had only been the beginning. Their children had grown and married and given them grandchildren to coddle and adore, and now here one of their grandbabies was to be wed.

"Tuck?" Eloise asked now, straightening. "Do you suppose we'll be great-grandparents soon?"

Tuck turned to her. "With the way that young man looks at our Ellen? We'll be great-grandparents before the year is out," he said triumphantly, and Eloise laughed.

She laughed for the wonder of it, this thing they had made together when they were never meant to be together at all. Love really did have a way of conquering everything.

But Tuck turned serious then, his brow furrowing. "Eloise, dear, you didn't tell the grandchildren the whole story of how we met. Did you?" he added questioningly.

She patted his arm reassuringly. "Don't worry, darling. I left out the details, just as we discussed."

She smiled right before he kissed her, this man she had loved for the whole of her life and then some.

ABOUT THE AUTHOR

Jessie decided to be a writer because there were too many lives she wanted to live to just pick one.

Taking her history degree dangerously, Jessie tells the stories of courageous heroines, the men who dared to love them, and the world that tried to defeat them.

Jessie lives in New Hampshire where if she is not at her desk writing, she's probably letting the dog out. Again.

For more, visit her website at jessieclever.com.

9 798988 191674